I0736600

HOW TO CATCH A RIVAL

SPECIAL EDITION

CHESTER FALLS
BOOK TWO

ANA ASHLEY

Illustrated by
COVERS BY JULES

How to Catch a Rival - Chester Falls Book 2
Original © 2020 by Ana Ashley
Special Paperback Edition: September 2023
ISBN-978-1-915031-06-8

How to Catch a Rival is a work of fiction. Names, characters, businesses, places events and incidents are either products of the author's imagination or used in a fictitious manner. Any resemblance to actual persons, living or dead, or actual events is purely coincidental.

Cover design: Covers by Jules

Editor: Alphabitz Editing

Join Ana's Facebook Group *facebook.com/groups/CafeRoMMance* for exclusive content, and to learn more about her latest books at *anawritesmm.com*!

DEDICATION

For those who walk the fine line between love and hate, and aren't afraid to take a detour.
Enjoy the adventure!

Ana

x

ABOUT HOW TO CATCH A RIVAL

When you're competing, the last thing you should do is fall in love…especially with your rival.

Wren turned up out of nowhere and now **he's my boss**…kind of. He's also a **straight**, closed-off, emotionless icicle. Who cares if he's also drop dead gorgeous, with eyes you could get lost in?

Tom is beautiful, colorful, strong, creative, and my eyes can't stop following him everywhere he goes. He also works for my parents, which means he's **off limits**. That, and I haven't told them that I'm bi yet.

A **baking competition** with high stakes

Two men who both need that prize money

When the heat moves from the kitchen to the bedroom, will Tom and Wren put their rivalry aside? Or is what they stand to lose more important than their growing feelings?

How to Catch a Rival is the second book in the Chester Falls series and features a larger-than-life sparkly character, two guys who can't deny their attraction, plenty of steam, fun and a guaranteed HEA.

TOM

"*Dress* shabbily and they remember the dress; dress impeccably and they remember the woman," I said to my reflection in the mirror. I was wearing a lavender three-piece suit that made my eyes pop. "Before you leave the house look in the mirror and take one thing off."

The words of my idol, Coco Chanel, never failed me, so I took off the handkerchief from the jacket lapel. I did a full turn for a final check and left my small apartment to go to work.

Maybe wearing a suit to work at Mason's general store would have been excessive for most people, but I refused to compromise, at least where it came to fashion.

One of my earliest memories was when I found my mom's pearls and spent hours in her room wrapping the long necklace around me. When she'd found me she sat on the floor next to me and had said, "This is how Coco would have worn her pearls," and then she'd opened a drawer in her chest and pulled out a box. For the rest of the afternoon we'd played together, wrapping and unwrapping her pearls around my neck, and till this day it was one of my favorite childhood memories.

I turned the corner into Chester Falls town square and opened the door of Spilled Beans to the sound of the jingling bell. In two months of living in Chester Falls, it never ceased to make me feel all warm and fuzzy inside.

"Morning, Tom," Indy, the barista, said.

There were three people in the line to get their morning coffee, and all three turned back, looked at me, and smiled.

"Hi, Indy, it's a gorgeous morning. Where are you taking us this week?"

"This week we're in Brazil, where the coffee beans grow at high altitude and have a sweet and full-bodied taste. You'll love it."

The pastry display was, as usual, full of delicious-looking sin. There was no point in trying to pretend to myself that I wasn't going to take one of Indy's cinnamon buns. I figured all the walking I did these days more than made up for the calorie intake.

As I waited for my turn in line, I looked out to the town square. The trees were turning into beautiful fall shades of dark reds, oranges, and browns. Beyond the square and right next to Bookmarked, the town's bookstore, was my dream— the empty store I hoped one day I could afford to lease.

"What's it going to be today, Tom? Mocha latte? Vanilla and cinnamon latte with a hint of pumpkin spice? What can I create for you?" Indy asked.

"Black, no cream, no sugar, and one of your cinnamon buns, please."

"You sure I can't interest you in something more creative?"

"I'm sure."

Indy shook his head and filled my reusable cup with his new Brazilian coffee.

I'd met Indy when my best friend Charlie had brought me to his hometown of Chester Falls a few months back. The first time I laid eyes on the indigo-haired barista I'd flirted shamelessly, and he'd flirted right back. Even now my cheeks heated a little at the thought.

When I'd returned to Chester Falls with Charlie, after another round of flirting, Indy and I had tried to hookup. I'd drank cocktails, he'd drank cocktails. I'd imagined running my fingers through his long hair, that was normally tied up in a bun, while he pushed his way inside of my tight heat. He'd imagined the same.

As they say, two bottoms don't a top make, and that had been the end of Tindy, as I'd called us in my head, and the start of a friendship. Or maybe we'd both known we would be better as friends and didn't want to ruin that with a meaningless hookup.

I picked up the small paper bag with the pastry and took a sip of the coffee. As Indy had said, it was sweet and full-bodied, and just what I needed.

"Indy, this coffee is great," I said, walking to the door. "See you tomorrow."

"One of these days I will convert you to my lattes."

"You'd have better luck converting me to a top," I teased before stepping out into the cool fall morning. I didn't miss the slight blush in Indy's cheeks.

I drank my coffee without rushing on my way to work. Walking past the empty store on my way to Mason's and staring at it for at least five minutes was part of my daily ritual now. I'd planned out in my head what it would look like, the colors, the furniture. Even the smallest details, like what kind of pictures would hang on the wall; it was all part of the dream.

When Charlie had told me he was moving out of our Boston apartment all the way to Lydovia to live with his boyfriend, Kris, I'd been so happy for him but also lost as to what to do.

Charlie had had his own fairy-tale love, meeting a real-life prince and falling in love. The press hadn't made it easy on them, and I'd witnessed firsthand how Charlie struggled with being in the public eye, but as they say, love conquers all, and so my best friend moved all the way to a different country.

At first I'd been determined to stay on my own in Boston. I'd picked up extra hours at work while I'd looked for a new roommate, but as the months had passed and I'd been no closer to finding someone to share the apartment with, I'd had to make some decisions.

"I can still pay my share of the bills," Charlie had said one weekend he'd visited with Kris.

"I know you're trying to pay me back for helping you see the hot piece of royal ass right in front of you, but that's what fairy godmothers do. Besides, I might find a new roommate soon."

Charlie had taken a leaf out of my book and had sat me down, made me an ultra-sweet cocktail, and told me he wasn't having any of it. I could accept his help with the bills or maybe consider a move.

The cocktail had been all kinds of awful, but in the sugar-induced coma I admitted moving out of Boston hadn't been something I had considered. After living in the city for so long, it hadn't crossed my mind that I could live elsewhere.

Moving back to Colorado to live near my mom had been out of the question. I loved her but I did not love the freezing winters.

One thing was certain, I was ready for a change.

When Charlie suggested I could move to Chester Falls, I'd dismissed it, but a few more cocktails in—this time prepared by me—I'd wanted my own prince, like Charlie, and I wanted to live in a tiny house, because they're super cool, and I wanted to be at one with nature.

Ben, the owner of Bookmarked, came out of his store to place his A-sign outside, which reminded me I needed to stop daydreaming and go to work.

"Morning, Tom, I see you're checking in on your baby."

"One day she'll be mine. Doesn't look like anyone wants her anyway," I said wistfully, looking through the large window and seeing the too-bare walls that needed all the love I had to give.

According to Ben, the store had been empty since the old lady who leased it had passed away a year ago.

"Maybe it's waiting for the right owner," Ben said, placing his hand on my shoulder.

"Yeah."

The walk to Mason's was an introspective one. It would take a long time to save enough money to open my fashion boutique, but I was determined to not let it get me down. I was already doing all the hours the Masons could afford to give me in their store, but I could still take another job.

I walked into Mason's through the back entrance, as usual, but unlike every day up till now, what greeted me wasn't a super-tidy storeroom with the office door at the back open where Jonas Mason, the owner, could ask me how everything was up front while I grabbed some stock for a customer.

No, the vision in front of me made my heart swell, and my creative brain exploded with sensory stimulation.

I navigated my way around the many boxes that over-flowed with decorations in all the colors of the rainbow, there were even rainbow cardboard cutouts and rainbow tinsel. There were also rolls of fabric and boxes of stock that were fortunately still sealed, because I wasn't sure anything in here would survive the glitter dust.

"What's going on?" I asked.

Abigail and Jonas Mason stood side by side with the biggest smiles on their faces.

"Tom, welcome to Chester Falls Pride month," they announced.

I remembered Charlie talking about the month-long Pride celebrations. Chester Falls took their support of the LGBTQ community seriously.

While most places celebrated fall and Halloween, Chester Falls did Pride in October. Now if that wasn't an omen for how much I belonged in this town, I didn't know what was.

"Abigail, Jonas, I'm about to jump out of my skin with happiness with all this color and trust me, if I wasn't wearing one of my best suits—my own creation by the way—I'd be on the floor playing already. Please tell me you'll let my little unicorn heart play with all of this." I sang.

"Abi," Jonas said, placing a soft kiss on Abigail's cheek. "I'll leave you two to it while I'm out front."

The look the older couple exchanged was so sweet. Thankfully, I could cope with all the happiness and glitter any time of day, even before nine in the morning.

"Right, my dear, we have a job to do."

"Let me put my things in the locker and I'll be all yours."

I had a feeling this would be a messy day, so I hung up my suit jacket and rolled up my sleeves, leaving the vest over my shirt.

"There's a window display competition every year during Pride month. We won it a few times before, but Trisha Potts from the haberdashery store has won the last five years in a row. Rumor has it she hires someone from New Haven to do her window. No one's been able to prove it. She normally covers up her window the day before Pride month starts, and the next morning it's all done."

I picked a few items from the boxes to see what we were working with. Some looked fairly old, but there was definitely potential. The general store sold a little of everything: small appliances, houseware, soft furnishings, and even locally sourced gift food like honey, jelly, and especially nutmeg and apple cider.

"Abigail, whatever Trisha has, she doesn't have a Tom Jones. This is going to be the best window display, and Mason's will bring that trophy back. Mark my words."

Maybe I was overly confident, but even though I spent my evenings designing and making clothes, it had been a while since I'd had a chance to show my creativity, and I was dying to get stuck into a new project.

"I knew I could count on you, dear. God knows neither of my sons have a creative bone in their body."

Sixteen-year-old Troy Mason often helped in the store. He was a nice kid, but he was more interested in computers and coding. It was thanks to him that Mason's had the best website I'd even seen from a small-town store.

I hadn't met the Mason's older son, Wren. Abigail had mentioned him a few times. He was some kind of hotshot footballer in California.

"So tell me, Tom. What are your thoughts for this window?"

"Come with me."

Abigail followed me out of the storeroom. My idea was to create a three-dimensional window display of a living room, showcasing the products from the store but also making it super fabulously full of color. I wanted understated glamor.

We didn't get to the window, because as we passed one of the many aisles in the store, Abigail suddenly stopped and let out a scream just as I saw Jonas Mason collapsed on the floor.

WREN

The twink trying to climb me like a tree was a sure bet, but the sexy girl with the red lipstick and the long dark hair leaning against the bar talking to her friend was doing it for me too. On nights like these I knew I'd be better going home alone and rubbing one off in the shower before going to bed.

"The team had a good start to the season, Coach Mason," Tracy, one of the teachers at school said. "The kids wouldn't shut up about last night's game long enough to focus in class today."

One knee injury and my pro-football career had been over just as it had been taking off. It was something I'd battled with initially because football had been my sole focus during those teenage years when I'd struggled to figure myself out, and the only thing that had ever made sense had been playing my favorite sport.

Having my dream end so abruptly had hurt more than the injury, but I'd found a new passion in teaching sports and coaching football. It didn't hurt that most teachers at my school were cool people, and the students didn't give me much grief.

"With all due respect, Trace, I wouldn't want to focus on geography either," Rob said.

Tracy punched Rob in the arm and he pretended to be hurt.

"What is it you teach again, Rob?" I asked, taking a sip of my beer.

"Fuck you, Mason."

"It's Wren, and it sounds like someone's math class lacked focus today too." I grinned as I raised my bottle in mock cheers and finished it off.

After my short-lived football career had ended, I couldn't face going back home, so I'd stayed in California.

Maybe I should go home on the next school break. Just for a few days. The last time my parents came to San Diego was five years back to watch my debut game with the San Diego Marinos, and it had been at least three years since I'd been home.

God, I missed Chester Falls. It had been too long since I'd done one of my favorite things: running in the forest outside Chester Falls followed by a hot shower and a slice of my mom's apple pie.

A pang of nostalgia hit me. Fuck, I needed to go home.

I almost didn't notice the twink's hand wandering up and down my leg, getting closer and closer to my crotch. The fact that I wasn't even hard was reason enough to call it a night and take my sullen mood home.

I grabbed the wrist of the guy, Stephen? Sean?

"I'm heading home, guys."

A chorus of groans followed my statement.

"Tell you what, you heathens, I'll buy you a round so you don't get sad without me here."

That was followed by cheers and raised glasses. I laughed and moved to get up, but Stephen, or Sean, tightened his hold on my thigh. I took his hand and pulled him toward the bar with me.

There was no need to let him down in front of everyone, and since he'd joined our group with the sole purpose of flirting with one of us, I hoped he'd either make his own way back to the table or pick someone else.

I asked the bartender for a round of drinks and then turned to him.

"Look—"

He put his hand up to stop me.

"Tonight's not my night, is it?" He had such a sweet smile, I was tempted to kiss him just to take away the sting of rejection.

"I'm sorry."

"That's okay." He shrugged. "You're still buying me a drink though because Sam here is going back to the table and flirt with Mr. Math teacher with the wandering eyes."

Sam, that was his name. I looked at the table and true enough, Rob was looking at us.

"Rob? He's straight as an arrow."

Sam laughed. "If you think he's straight then you need to give back your gay card, honey."

The bartender put all the drinks on the bar and I slipped him a few notes to cover the check and tip, and then I gave Sam a kiss on the cheek and whispered in his ear, "I'm not gay, I'm bi."

He chuckled and took the drinks back to the table as I left the bar. I didn't miss Rob's smile as Sam took the drinks back. I really hadn't seen that one coming, then again, Rob was new at the school and had only been out with us a few times.

When I got home, I turned the TV onto a sports channel and headed for the shower.

As the water cascaded down my body, I wondered if the reason for my introspective mood was that the team had started the season on such a high, and that was making me anxious.

It was always challenging to keep the momentum going. You win a lot and people expect you to keep winning, but if you lose a game, they ditch you like you can never recover from it. I always preferred to see a mix of wins and losses early in the season. It kept the kids on their toes, and the final win would taste so much better.

I planned out in my head the bones of my strategy for the next couple of training sessions to throw the team off. It was a gamble, and we could lose a game or two, but I knew it was the best long-term strategy.

My cock hardened as I ran soap through it. Yes, I was one of those guys who got hard thinking of football. It was the adrenaline, the excitement of thinking about a game, feeling invincible on the field. Even though I wasn't playing it professionally anymore, football was still in my blood.

I ignored my cock's pleas and finished the shower quickly, settling in front of the TV for a couple of mind-numbing hours before going to bed.

When I woke up the next morning, I had the usual text waiting for me.

Aiden: *Run.*

My best friend Aiden's texts always lacked enough words, but I did need a run this morning, so I got up, got my running gear on, and left to meet him in the usual parking lot.

"How's it going?" I asked as we did a slow jog to the sidewalk running alongside the beach.

"Same same."

I looked at Aiden. My frown must have given me away because he frowned back.

"What's up, Aid?"

"Nothing. Had an argument with Richard last night, and when I woke up he wasn't home. He probably went to the gym or something. He always does that when we argue."

"What did you argue about?"

"Same as always, money."

Aiden came from a super-wealthy family but was the most down-to-earth person I'd ever met. He refused to use his family's money or influence, something that was a bone of contention with his boyfriend Richard, the dick.

It wasn't my place to tell Aiden to dump the money-hungry jackass, so I simply put my hand on his shoulder and picked up my pace.

I'd met Aiden when I'd started running after recovering from my injury. We'd always run the same path and parked near each other. Even though Aiden had a more reserved personality, I'd needed a running buddy and had decided Aiden was going to be it. The rest of our friendship built naturally from that moment on.

We ran side by side, the only sounds the ones coming from our running shoes on the wide footpath and our heavy breathing. I needed the feeling of pushing my body to that point where the only thing going through my mind was how I was going to cope with the next mile.

It wasn't until we were almost back at the parking lot and winding down from the run that Aiden broke the silence. He looked a little more out of breath than usual.

"So, you gonna tell me what's bothering you?"

"Nothing's bothering me, what do you mean?"

"You were pounding the sidewalk as if your legs have an expiration date," he said.

"Man, don't even joke about that."

"You know I didn't mean it like that, but you were clearly trying to outrun something. How about we grab a coffee and talk about it?"

I nodded.

The last mile was painful despite the slow jog. My knee started aching, which was a sure sign I'd overdone it again. I'd been good with my recovery, making sure I could still be active, but occasionally, when I took my frustrations out on the sidewalk, I always paid for it with a swollen knee and a few days' rest.

It was still early in the day but warm enough to sit outside the coffee shop. The bitter taste of the coffee and the warmth of the sun on my face was the perfect combination for post-run pick-me-up.

"Here."

I opened my eyes to see Aiden holding a bag of ice. He maneuvered one of the spare chairs in front of me, and I lifted my leg to rest on the chair, placing the ice on it.

"Fuck, that's cold."

"I believe that's how ice works," Aiden said. "Now, talk time."

I chuckled. Aiden was the least bossy person I knew. Even as he was telling me what to do, I could see his concern that I'd pushed myself too far today. I couldn't disagree with him.

"I'm not sure what to tell you, Aid. Recently I've just been feeling a little out of sorts. I miss home, miss proper seasons, the forest air, my family."

The sea was calm this morning, a contrast to how I was feeling inside. I stared at it, trying to channel the peace I needed.

"How about having a break? When was the last time you went home?"

"Too long ago," I confessed.

"Why don't you take some time off then?"

"It's complicated."

Aiden waved his hand. "My family doesn't approve of my chosen career, and they disapprove even more that I won't accept their money. Let's not even start on me being gay. My life is the definition of complicated."

"At least your family know who you are."

"What do you mean?"

"Yesterday, I met a guy. Really cute and up for some fun, but I couldn't find the energy to go through the motions of a hookup."

"You could try dating people properly for a change. But you still haven't answered my question."

I knew Aiden hadn't meant it as a dig. More than anyone, he knew I wanted to settle down, but he didn't know what it meant if I ended up wanting a guy instead of a woman.

When I'd got picked by the Marinos, I hadn't wanted to ruin my chances of a career in professional football by coming out. Not that my teammates were homophobic. Some were the best allies and worked hard raising money for local LGBTQ causes. I'd felt like a fraud next to them and had always joined in their fundraisers, but it hadn't taken away from the fear of not being picked by future teams because of my sexual orientation.

"My parents don't know about my injury, or that I don't play anymore," I confessed.

I couldn't look at Aiden because I knew he'd offer me comfort I wasn't sure I deserved.

"They also think I'm straight."

After a moment of silence, I couldn't help it. I turned to

face Aiden, flinching as my knee ached under the melting bag of ice.

"So, let me get this straight," he said. "Sorry, no pun intended."

I couldn't help laughing because Aiden's face was so serious.

"Your parents think you still play football, and you can't date anyone properly in case you fall in love with a man and have to come out to your parents?"

"Pretty much."

"I agree, it's complicated."

I wasn't sure if he was going to part some words of wisdom that I needed to come clean to my parents, but my cellphone rang in that moment, pausing the conversation. My brother's name flashed across the screen.

"Hey, little bro, what's up?"

"Wren, um...can you come home?"

I straightened my back at the sound of Troy's quiet voice.

"What happened? Are you okay?"

"It's Dad. He's in the hospital, he had a heart attack."

I gripped my phone tight, trying to keep my reaction calm for my brother.

"Is Dad..."

"He's in surgery at the moment. Mom didn't want me to call you until Dad was out but... I'm sorry, Wren, I'm so scared." My chest felt tight as I struggled to take in the fear in my little brother's voice.

Even though the sun was warm I felt cold all over. What if my dad didn't make it?

"It'll be okay, Troy, Dad is strong. I'm going to get a flight out as soon as I can, okay?"

"Thanks, Wren. Can't wait to see you."

"You too, little bro."

I nearly jumped when Aiden touched my arm.

"What's up?" he asked.

"Looks like I'm going home sooner than I thought," I said.

TOM

"Good morning, Mrs. Harris. How did you get on with the easy peeler?"

The sweet old lady had been a customer of Mason's for years and wouldn't trust any other retailer. Only a few days ago we'd spent an enormous amount of time going over the different vegetable peeling tools Mason's sold to find one that would make it easy on her arthritis.

"Oh, dear, it's fantastic. I can go back to making my apple pie now that I don't have any trouble peeling the apples. Speaking of which, I made one yesterday for Abi and Jonas."

Mrs. Harris placed a cake carrier on the countertop. How she'd even carried the thing all the way here with her walker, I didn't know.

"Thank you so much, Mrs. Harris. That's really kind of you. I'll put it out back for Abi."

"Tell her my thoughts and prayers are with her and poor Jonas. Let's hope for a speedy recovery."

"I'll make sure to tell her, Mrs. Harris."

She went to browse the store while I took the delicious-looking apple pie to the office where I'd stored the other cakes, pies, and food brought by the people of Chester Falls and loyal customers of Mason's.

I'd thought this stuff only happened in movies, but the evidence was in the overflowing staff fridge that had more food than the Masons could eat in one week. Considering Jonas had had a heart attack, I was certain Abi would intercept all the sugary treats anyway.

Fortunately, the well-wishers stopped coming in by lunchtime, so I grabbed my lunch and sat on a high stool behind the checkout counter. We had a nice staff area at the back where I usually took my break, but since I was on my own, I didn't want to close the store, and I was sure Abi wouldn't mind if I was discreet enough.

There were no customers in the store, so I took out the sandwich I'd prepared at home and the coffee Indy had put in a flask for me.

The bitter but smooth taste of Indy's Brazilian coffee couldn't have come at a better time. After the events of the day before, I was exhausted, but I also wanted to keep things going in the store for Abi, who was still with Jonas in the hospital.

When we'd seen Jonas collapsed on the floor yesterday, somehow the first aid training I'd received at my old job at Clarence's department store had kicked in and I'd asked Abi to call an ambulance while I'd checked on Jonas.

He hadn't been breathing when I'd kneeled next to him, so I'd started CPR. I'd had no time to feel nervous or unsure. My actions could have been the difference between Jonas's life and death, and I hadn't wanted to think of the possibility of the latter.

The ambulance had arrived minutes later, but it had felt like hours when all my breaths and chest compressions hadn't seemed like they were having any effect on Jonas.

When the paramedics had used the defibrillator on Jonas's

chest, his body had finally responded. I don't think I'd taken a breath until the medic had said they had a beat. Abi had clung onto me so tight our joined hands were white.

As I couldn't go with her in the ambulance, I'd offered to keep the store open and made her promise to keep me updated. I'd kept myself busy dusting shelves and restocking while I'd waited for news.

The display window had remained untouched for the rest of the day, and I hadn't felt I should plan anything before I knew Jonas was awake and in recovery. Knowing me, it would end up being more a sad window than a Pride, happy one.

After waiting for news for the rest of the day, Abi had finally called in the morning to tell me Jonas had had emergency surgery on his heart. He wasn't awake yet, but the surgery had been successful, and he was being monitored closely.

Troy came in just as I finished my sandwich.

"Hey, Troy, any news on your dad?"

The kid looked tired but his smile told me he had good news.

"Yeah, Dad woke up this morning. Mom said I could skip school today but asked me to come see if you were okay."

"Everything's under control here. How's she holding up?"

"She's okay now. It was bad yesterday, but now Dad's awake she's better," he said, leaning against the counter.

"There's a load of food in the fridge, if you want to take some home with you."

Troy laughed. "Did Mrs. Perkins bring a cheesecake?"

"I'm not sure which customer is Mrs. Perkins but there's at least three cheesecakes. Who brings cheesecake to sick people?"

"Right? When Mom hurt her back last year, they thought me and Dad would starve to death so everyone kept bringing food every day. We had to refuse and give some to the neighbors because we couldn't eat it all."

"Well, in that case I might take some home with me tonight."

Troy nodded and went to the back office.

I pulled out the notebook where I'd been sketching my ideas for the Pride window. Now more than ever I wanted Mason's to win the Pride window competition, so I scanned over my notes and made some more.

Troy came back minutes later holding a few containers of food.

"Here," I said, taking a Mason's shopping bag from under the counter and giving it to Troy for the boxes.

"Thanks. Oh, Wren is coming from California, so I guess he'll be around to help a little while Mom is in the hospital with Dad."

I hadn't met the elusive older son of the Masons'. Hadn't even seen a photo. But if he had the same gentle manner the rest of the family had, I was sure I wouldn't have any trouble working with him in the store.

After closing up I distracted myself with the Pride window plans, and didn't leave until nearly nine o'clock. As I walked past Spilled Beans I saw Indy through the window and wondered if he was up for sharing dinner.

"We're only open for broken hearts," Indy said when the door bells gave my presence away. He didn't even turn from where he was cleaning the coffee maker.

"How about for a free dinner?"

"Lock the door behind you and tell me what you're offering."

"I'm not sure, you know. I think it's some kind of casserole."

All the chairs were upside down on top of the tables, so I picked the table closest to the counter and pulled the chairs back down, using one to hang my burgundy suit jacket on. Today I'd kept my look simple. I wore jeans and a white shirt, all perfectly fitted, of course.

I handed the casserole dish to Indy so he could reheat it in the oven and went behind the counter to fix us a drink.

"Do you remember the first time I came here and took over your drinks?" I asked.

Indy had given me a lecture about not stepping into his space. I'd sat and listened and then I'd asked him to try the cocktail I'd prepared for him.

"That was before I knew you had magic hands."

I quirked an eyebrow, which he caught as he was coming out of the kitchen area.

"I'm dead on my feet today so you're having water, or whatever you have in the chiller," I said.

"Water is fine, thanks."

Indy sat down with a giant sigh and propped his legs up on a spare chair. I knew it was hard to be on my feet all day in the store, but the pace at Spilled Beans was relentless. I didn't know how Indy did it, and always with a genuine smile.

"So, to what do I owe the pleasure of this visit?" he asked. "Not that I'm not thankful for the food and all."

He sat up and put his hand to his chest. "This is a broken-hearts visit, isn't it? Tell me, who is he, and we'll fix you right up."

"I really have no idea what you're talking about, but now you've mentioned this broken-heart thing twice I need to know."

"Ah, it's nothing. Sometimes people come here as I'm

closing and they like to chat. It's always about some kind of matter of the heart. I keep telling them I'm a barista not a therapista, but..." He shrugged.

The oven dinged and Indy moved to get up, but I gestured for him to stay where he was. I plated the food and brought it out. My belly rumbled at the lovely smell, reminding me I hadn't eaten since my sandwich earlier on.

Indy released his dark-blue hair from the elastic band that kept it up while he worked and dug into the food.

"Hmm, I love Momma Ruth's casserole."

"How do you know who made it?"

"Have you been to Benny's yet?"

I shook my head. Chester Falls wasn't a big town, but it seemed there was still plenty I hadn't seen.

"You have to go there. Momma Ruth is the best cook in town. How did you get this if you didn't go to Benny's?"

"People have been bringing food for Abi and Jonas all day. I've lost track of who brought what, but now that you mention it, I remember a girl coming in wearing a yellow shirt with a badge that had the name Benny's on it. All I kept thinking was how the color made her look washed out. She's meant to be in bright-green clothes that complement her light complexion."

Indy looked at me, shaking his head and bringing his hands up to massage his scalp. His hair was long and wavy. It was a shame it lived constrained by the elastic band, but I couldn't deny Indy rocked the man-bun look better than anyone I'd ever seen.

"Trust you to do a fashion makeover in your head when someone's handing you food."

"It's in my blood. Can't help it."

I looked out toward my store and imagined what it would be like to stay late making sure everything looked beautiful or doing the window display. No, it wasn't my store. Yet. But I prayed to Coco and all the rainbow fairies out there, it would be one day.

I gazed over to a poster on the wall I hadn't seen before.

"Oh, what's that?"

Indy followed my line of sight and then got up to go behind the counter, bringing back what looked like a smaller version of the poster.

"You know about the Pride festival, right?"

"Yes, I'm working on a window display for the Masons."

"There are lots of events, but the one that people love the most, with exception of parade day, is the Pride bake-off."

I read the information on the leaflet. The competition was for amateur bakers, and there was a prize.

"Fuck me," I said out loud. "Ten thousand dollars?"

"Yup, it's insane. People raise money all year round for the prize because the competition is so much fun to watch. They do the challenges in the high school gym hall. Last year, one contestant set her hair on fire when she was doing a crème brûlée. Another one forgot to turn the oven on. You'd have thought the lack of heat from the oven was a giveaway, but no, she still took the cake out and turned it onto a plate. The batter went everywhere, and then she slipped on it, and as she was falling over she took another contestant down with her."

By the time he finished, tears were running down Indy's face, but my gaze kept going back to the prize money on the piece of paper I was holding.

Ten thousand dollars plus the savings I already had would be enough to lease the store for a year.

"Indy," I said, looking back up, not quite believing what I was about to ask. "I think I'm going to enter this bake-off. Will you help me?"

WREN

It had been three years since I'd seen my family, and looking at my dad's sleeping form on the hospital bed, I knew it had been too long. Hell, even a year would have been too long.

He looked like he'd aged ten years, which was likely a result of his heart attack and being unwell, but the light-gray hair on the sides of his head hadn't shown up overnight.

That much was evidence that life had carried on for my parents in my absence. They were both in their mid-fifties. The store kept them busy and active, but was it starting to be too much for them? Was work what had caused my dad's heart attack?

I wouldn't know because I hadn't been around, I hadn't visited; I hadn't asked.

My dad stirred a little, so I pulled the hard plastic hospital chair closer to his bed, sat down again, and held his hand. His skin was soft, small wrinkles were showing his age, but what really got to me was how pale he was.

After Troy's call I'd looked for flights on my cellphone, but

"

my hands had been too shaky. Aiden had taken the phone from me and within a few minutes he'd booked me on the next available flight.

I hadn't even called the school to see if they could find cover first. Luckily, the principal was very sympathetic and told me to take as long as I needed.

Another call to the assistant coach on my way to the airport a few hours later, and he'd taken down my plans for the team's training and next couple of games.

I could stay in Chester Falls for at least the next three weeks, but now, seeing my dad lying on the hospital bed looking so frail, I wasn't sure it would be enough. If it would ever be enough, but those were thoughts to pack away for another day.

When I'd arrived at the hospital my mom had told me he'd been in surgery for the best part of the day before and had woken up briefly before I arrived. I'd only just missed Troy, who'd gone back home to rest since he had to go back to school tomorrow.

That was another thing to add to the guilt I was already feeling. It was my sixteen-year-old brother that had been here for our parents. I rested my head on my arms without letting go of my dad's hand.

Tears I couldn't stop soaked the fabric of my shirt as tiredness came over me. I must have been really jetlagged because the next thing I was aware of was a hand running through my hair softly and whispered voices.

I looked up and met my dad's eyes.

"Dad, you're awake." My raspy, sleepy voice sounded foreign even to my ears.

My mom, who'd gone out to get us some coffee earlier, was back and sitting on the other side of the bed.

"Hey, Son."

"You know, Mom would have given you a vacation if you'd asked for it," I teased, not feeling the lightness I tried to show.

"What, this one?" he said, holding my mom's hand. "She's a slave driver. The other day even made me wash the dishes."

Like me, my mom's fake look of indignation wasn't selling it.

We'd had a talk outside the room when I'd arrived. It had been a very close call for my dad. The fact that he'd nearly died on the operation table twice was cause enough to take his recovery seriously and appreciate that he'd been extremely lucky. We had to count our blessings that we still had him with us.

"Mr. Mason," a nurse said, coming into the room. "I'm glad to see you awake. You gave us a little scare yesterday."

She checked him and injected something in his IV and made some notes on the file at the end of the bed. "How are you feeling?"

"Not running any marathons today, I can tell ya that," Dad said.

"Good to know, I need you to rest up and press the buzzer if you're in any pain. There are no heroes in here. If you're in pain, we can give you the good stuff, alright?"

"Yes, ma'am."

The nurse put a hand on my mom's shoulder and squeezed gently and smiled at me before leaving the room.

"What a pretty young lady," Dad said. "Did you see her smile at our boy, Abi?"

"Dad!"

"Leave it with me, Son, I'll be here a few days, I'll see what information I can get."

He winked and my mom shook her head.

I groaned. Trust him to think about my love life not five minutes after coming back from a life-changing operation. He turned to Mom and smiled; his eyes looked heavy.

"Sleep some more, my love," she said, placing her hand on his head and running her fingers through his hair.

I left the room to give my parents a moment together. In all the years I'd dated women, and more recently men, I'd never met anyone that made me feel anything close to what I saw between my parents when they looked at each other.

Movement in the nurses' station caught my eye, and I saw the nurse. She smiled the same warm smile from earlier when I approached.

"Hi, I'm Wren Mason, Jonas's son?"

"Oh yes, he should be sleeping soon from the medication I gave him, can I help you with anything?"

She started to get up from her chair so I held up my hand to stop her.

"No, no. He's fine. I wanted to ask you some questions, if that's okay."

"Of course. It's normal for families to want to know what happens next, the risks and so on. Mr. Mason had a major operation yesterday but he's a strong man."

"Thank you, he's also not the most patient man when it comes to being stuck in one place so I'm apologizing in advance."

She smiled again at my comment.

"Don't you worry, I've seen plenty of patients like your dad. Trust me, he's not too bad."

"When do you think he'll be released to go home?"

"It's hard to say because the next forty-eight hours are crucial, but he's doing well so far, so I think the doctors will probably release him in a week."

My mom came out of the room looking exhausted.

"Come here," I said, pulling my mom into my arms for a tight hug. She was small in my arms but not fragile. My mom was one of those women with inner strength you could see by just staring at her. She could deal with this and more. but I'd be damned if I didn't want to make it easier for her, even if it was just for a little while.

"Can I convince you to come home for some rest?"

She stood back and looked toward the door of my dad's room.

I could have kissed the nurse when she said, "The medication he's on will knock him out at least until tomorrow. Go home, Mrs. Mason. I'm on tonight's shift. I'll keep an eye on him and promise to call if anything changes."

My mom went over to the nurse and took both of the nurse's hands into hers. "Thank you, my dear. I really can't thank you enough for all your work."

Traffic out of the city was slow. I looked at my mom and noticed her staring at me.

"What?" I asked, taking her hand and bringing it up to my lips for a kiss.

"I missed you, that's all, it's been such a long time."

"I know, Mom. I guess I got so caught up with stuff I didn't realize how long it's been since I was home."

She smiled softly, her eyes boring into me as though she could read me like an open book.

"I'm staying for a little while to help out," I said.

"Oh no, my dear. You don't need to do that. You must be busy back in California. It was nice of you to come, but honestly, we'll be okay."

"I'm sorry, Mom." All the words I wanted to say were caught in my throat. At any other time, the slow-moving traffic would have been the ideal opportunity to open up to her.

Ever since I was a kid, and even before Troy was born and life at home had become busier for her, the time to really get my mom's undivided attention was when we were stuck somewhere. At first it had been when she drove me to school on rainy or snowy days, when it wasn't safe to walk. Then it had been after shutting the store, when my dad had been in the office cashing up and Mom and I had been out on the floor in semi-darkness, tidying up the shelves and bringing stock out.

Yes, this was the best opportunity, but not the best time.

"What are you sorry for?"

"Never mind, we can talk later. So, tell me what's new in Chester Falls."

The rest of the drive was taken up with the lowdown on my hometown. I was glad to know some things never changed. Benny's Diner was still there and going strong, and I couldn't wait to have one of Momma Ruth's pancake breakfasts.

"Isn't the Pride festival coming up soon?"

I saw my mom's face turning toward me from the corner of my eye.

"Yes, it starts next week."

"Are they still doing the window display contests?"

My mom crossed her arms and huffed.

"Yes. Although sometimes I don't know why we bother entering. We end up doing it more for the community than the competition."

I took a quick glance at her. Other families fussed over Thanksgiving, Christmas, Easter, but in our family it was all about the Pride festival and, in particular, the window competition. We'd even won it a few times, but I'd have to admit I hadn't given it much thought since I'd left for college as I had never been able to come back for the festival.

"You don't seem very enthusiastic about it."

She sighed. "I can't see past this week and getting your dad home. Tom is doing his best looking after the store, but I'm not sure he'll have enough time to work on the window because Troy's exams at school means he won't be around as much to help out."

"Who's Tom?"

"Oh, he's new in town. Such a sweetheart, he is, and hard-working too. Very creative. We hired him thinking Dad and I could step back a little, you know."

Yes, I knew. Working six days a week, covering the opening hours plus all the stuff that needed doing when the store was shut was hard work.

Mason's had always been a family business, and my parents instilled in us pride for the store, for the work we did, and the community. Can't say I was overjoyed to spend all the school vacations working, but it had taught me the discipline and routine I needed to succeed working in a team.

I was happy that my parents had already thought of stepping back a little, but a strange feeling settled in my chest at the thought there was someone working in the store that wasn't family.

Not that I could blame my parents for getting help when I wasn't around. God, I was such a jackass, but I wanted to do my part now I was in town, even if for a short time.

As we pulled into my parents' driveway and I stared at the house I grew up in, a sudden feeling of happiness settled in me. It was nice to be home.

"Mom," I said before we left the car. "I really do want to help. Let's have some rest and you can take me to the store in the morning for a handover before you go back to the hospital."

"Okay, dear. If you're sure."

"I'm sure. That Tom kid might be a good helper, but I

grew up in the store. You won't need to worry about anything for the next three weeks, okay?"

She looked at me like she was going to say something, but she simply smiled and stroked my cheek the way she always had when I was a kid.

"Okay."

TOM

After my evening with Indy I hadn't been able to stop thinking about the Pride bake-off. What was already a late evening had turned into an almost all-nighter when I'd got home, because I hadn't been able to stop researching everything I could about baking competitions, recipes, and especially getting acquainted with the rules of this particular competition.

I'd picked an outfit that I knew always made me feel good—a pink pair of jeans matched with a yellow shirt—and because I'd planned to work on the Pride window today, I also wore my yellow rainbow sweater. Charlie had given me the sweater for my birthday a couple of years ago after I'd broken up with my then boyfriend, and the little sparkly rainbows never failed to cheer me up.

Even my outfit hadn't hidden how tired I was, or maybe Indy just knew me that well because he'd put an extra shot of espresso in my morning coffee and had let me borrow his bigger flask for coffee for my lunch.

Mason's hadn't had any deliveries this morning and,

thankfully, people had stopped coming by with food, so I was able to work on the window. I wanted it to be an experience rather than something just for show.

Mason's was all about the community. I'd heard about the charity work Abi and Jonas had done over the years, so I wanted the window to be about bringing the community in and experience what it was to be part of the Mason family. I sent Troy a text asking for his help and then started restocking the homeware shelves.

I was carrying a few throws when a half-shrieky and full-annoying voice stopped me halfway down the aisle.

"Is Abi here?"

Turning around was a mistake because I couldn't stop my reaction to the hideous outfit the woman was wearing. Hoping I disguised my gag reflex with a cough, I put on my biggest smile.

Goodness gracious Coco. The woman's clothes fully matched her voice. Loud, mismatched, and my instinct told me to be more careful approaching her than a deadly spider.

"Good morning, I'm afraid Mrs. Mason isn't here today, can I help at all?"

"I want to speak to Abi, when is she back?"

"I'm not sure when Mrs. Mason will return from her errands, but if there's anything you need I'm happy to look for it in the storeroom or order it."

She sneered.

"I don't want anything from here."

The woman turned to leave just as Abi came out from the office area. She looked tired, like she hadn't slept for weeks, even though it had been only two days since Jonas's heart attack.

Despite the woman's presence, Abi sent me a smile before turning to the annoying woman.

"Hi, Trisha, how can I help?"

"Oh, hi, Abigail. I wanted to know if you're going to participate in the Pride window competition this year."

So, this was the infamous Trisha Potts, the woman from the haberdashery store. I turned back to place the throws on the shelf but kept my ears well-tuned in Abi and Trisha's direction.

If the woman so much as upset a hair on Abi's head, I'd pounce on her like a tiger, and even fear of snagging my favorite sweater on her claws wouldn't stop me.

Fortunately, Trisha didn't stay long, and Abi didn't look like she needed help handling her.

There was a small breeze from the door as a new customer came in. I moved to greet them, but as I went around the aisle I stopped in my tracks, because right in front of me was the chest of my dreams.

The white shirt did a poor job of hiding the rock-hard muscles underneath. I took in a shallow breath and a waft of unmistakable woodsy citrus assaulted my senses.

"Bleu by Chanel," I whispered.

I was almost afraid of looking up in case the face that went with the body and the heavenly smell didn't quite match, even though I partly doubted it, and partly didn't care.

Eyes bluer than the sky, blond hair that was short on the sides and longer on top, just long enough to fall a little to the sides, and I wondered what it would feel like to tug on it as the full lips attached to that sinful mouth wrapped around my cock.

"Are you okay?"

The voice was rich and deep but soft, and it spoke right into my soul.

"Holy mother of fairies, are you real?"

There was no doubt I was hallucinating. Maybe I'd hit my

head on a shelf and didn't realize I'd knocked myself out. I really should touch it to make sure.

My eyes were fixed on my hand as I raised it slowly and saw the chest expand and deflate in rapid succession. He radiated heat, like real-life warmth, but before I could feel it under my touch he grabbed my wrist.

"What are you doing?"

The cold tone of the voice made me look up again. The words dagger and ice came to mind.

I stepped away from him and nearly tripped on a stool I used to reach the higher shelves. Quickly, I recovered, dusting off my stupidity and standing as tall as my five feet ten allowed.

"I'm sorry, I think I was possessed by a spirit but it has left me now. How can I help?"

The space between his eyebrows narrowed. His eyes flickered between my mouth and my eyes. Oh crap, maybe he was deaf. I repeated my words again but slowly in case he could read my lips.

"Hooow. Caaan. I. Heeelp?"

"I should be asking you that. Are you looking for anything in particular? Something for the house, a gift?"

"You're not deaf?"

"No."

"Oh, thank god. My ASL is limited to asking for a Snarky Hyena at the Compass, because the bartender is *très mignon*."

"You...what...where...huh?"

"A Snarky Hyena. It won't get you drunk but it'll make you so so happy."

"What are you?"

His question was like a bucket of ice-cold water on me. When the cold-water challenge did the rounds a few years ago Charlie and I had joined in with our department at work.

Despite raising a lot of money for charity, I'd hated doing the challenge. But somehow, having a real bucket of water on me didn't make me feel as cold as this guy's words.

I'd thought the days of coming across straight guys who thought they could catch the gay from me were mostly gone, but, sometimes, one of those rare birds flew too close to the sun. And I knew just how to singe their wings.

"Oh, honey, no need to hurt your pretty little head trying to figure out complex biology." My voice sounded sickeningly sweet, even to my ears.

I took one step forward and this time my hands did land on his chest, but unlike before, my eyes didn't leave his. His chest was warm and hard as I'd suspected, and I tried to ignore how good it felt, and how it would be if he used his strong arms to keep me safe from the world.

Any other time I'd have allowed time to stand still as I explored the Adonis under my touch, but this wasn't one of those. This was a game, and one I needed to win. *Get your head in it, Tom. The right head.*

"Don't give yourself an aneurism, sweetie. I like to keep the gay to myself, it's more fun that way."

He laughed. He actually laughed.

I was ready to show him my claws when we were interrupted and I realized I was at work. Fuck!

"That woman brings out feelings in me I never thought I'd have for another human being. And not the good kind, if you know what I mean," Abi said, approaching me.

If the customer complained about me I'd certainly lose my job. Why couldn't I ever keep my mouth shut?

Frozen in my spot, I didn't know if I should greet Abi or try to turn things around with the customer. After all, beastly customers were good customers if they were paying customers. I repeated the mantra in my head and turned to the guy with my best customer service smile.

He wasn't looking at me anymore, and for a split second I missed his gaze on me. Maybe I was hungry. Yes, that would explain it.

Then I noticed he was focused on Abi with an expression of adoration.

"I see you two have met," Abi said.

"What?" we both said at the same time.

"Tom, this is my son Wren." And then she turned to Wren. "Honey, this is Tom, my lifesaver in this store and the angel that kept your dad alive until the paramedics arrived."

Her voice wobbled a little, and as the feelings of helplessness from the other day came back to me, I hugged her tight.

"How is he doing?"

She cleared a tear that escaped her eyes. "He's doing better than expected, but we nearly lost him. I can't even begin to imagine if..."

"Shhh," I said, running my hands up and down her arms. "He's strong. Just tell him there's about a million pies in the fridge waiting for him, and you'll see him run out of that hospital in no time."

She shook her head. "He's going to be on a strict diet from now on. So help me god, if I find another stash of jelly beans hiding in the house when he's back home."

We all laughed, which only meant that Jonas's best-kept secret had never been a secret.

"Anyway, you kept this hunk away from me," I said. "Why have we not got any posters of him bare-chested in the storeroom? Can I play with him? Is he mine to keep?" I batted my eyelashes at her and she laughed. I didn't miss the severe angry look that Wren was throwing my way. One that I totally chose to ignore.

"You'll have plenty of time to play together," she said. "Wren is staying home for the next few weeks to help out in the store so I can focus on Jonas."

I put my hands together in a prayer gesture. "I'm so going to light a candle to my fairy godmother when I get home tonight."

Fuck.

The words out of my mouth didn't match the mortification I felt inside. Not only had I made a fool of myself by behaving like a nymphomaniac hitting on a straight man, he was also my boss's son, and kind of my boss too now he was working in the store.

And because he hadn't so much as uttered a word to me in the time Abi was introducing us, I did what Tom does.

"I think you should come round my place later and I'll work all that tension out of you. What you need is a deep shoulder massage and a Tom cocktail." I winked. "I'll even let you pick the ratio of cock to tail."

Abi shook her head again and looked at Wren who, despite the stern face, had a cute blush rising from the collar of his shirt. I wondered if Abi had seen it.

"You're barking up the wrong tree, my dear," Abi said.

"I don't want to bark at it, Abi. I want to climb it."

Wren picked that moment to leave us. I hadn't even noticed the customers were hovering by the checkout waiting to pay for their goods. Wren smiled at the customers. Something churned in my stomach. Damn it, I really needed to eat something.

The first thing I did when I got home was to enroll in the Pride bake-off. Now, more than ever, I needed to win that competition, because I was absolutely, one hundred percent sure that at some point in the near future I would do something that would cause Wren to complain about me and get me fired.

What was it about the man that got all my feathers ruffled?

It was strange being back home.

The space above the garage had been converted into a fully contained guest apartment and even had its own separate entrance. This had been one of the projects my dad had promised to work on but had never got to it before I left for college.

My mom didn't say when it had been done and dismissed it as just something they did so my aunt who lived in Colorado could visit, but I wondered if underneath it all they'd hoped I'd one day come home, or at least visit more.

Having the privacy the apartment afforded me was a plus, considering I'd fully expected to go back to my childhood bedroom, except it had been turned into a study room for Troy. A study room that looked more like NASA's mission control.

Troy had always been interested in gadgets, electronic stuff, and then as he'd got older it was computers. I'd always suspected he would end up doing something in that area so I was more than happy to see my old room transformed to allow my younger brother to work on his computer stuff.

When I'd arrived home from the hospital Troy had been studying for a test. He'd given me a half-apology for taking up my room but had then started talking about all the cool stuff he could do with his computers, and within a minute I'd had him in a headlock and had ruffled his hair like I used to do when he was younger.

Mom had caught us and half-heartedly told us off, but I could tell she was happy to have us all home. I just hoped my dad would be able to join us soon. I knew I wouldn't go back to San Diego until I'd had a chance to spend some time with him too. As it was, I already had too many regrets.

One of them was how disconnected I was from the family business.

We'd always expected that I wouldn't follow in my parents' footsteps because of my interest in sports, but Mason's had been in the family for four generations and it was part of who I was.

I remembered Mason's as the store that sold a little bit of everything. The one-stop store for the people of Chester Falls, and often it was where they stopped even when they didn't need more than a chat and sharing the local gossip.

Walking back into the store had been surreal. So much was the same but also totally different.

The storeroom was full of boxes of decorations for the Pride window. My mom had told me they'd got them all out the day Dad had had the heart attack, and it looked like nothing had been done with them since.

The office was the same mess I remembered, and I was pretty sure if I lifted some of the paperwork, I'd find invoices going back a few years. "It's an organized mess," my dad always said. And true to his word, whenever you asked him about anything he always knew where it was.

Now the desk was also occupied by a number of cakes, and

when I dared look inside the small fridge I saw it had enough cheesecake and food to feed a battalion. Who brings cheesecake to a sick man, anyway?

It had taken a while over dinner the night before to convince my mom that I wasn't compromising on my stay. I wanted to help out, and I would stay as long as it was needed and run the store while she focused on Dad.

She was worried about all the games and training I'd miss while I was in Chester Falls and reassured me that Tom was a great help already. Troy had looked at me, but I couldn't tell what he was thinking. I'd simply told her not to worry about it.

My first job in the store was to introduce myself to the man who'd not only saved my dad but had kept everything going in my parents' absence. Both Mom and Troy wouldn't stop talking about Tom: how helpful he was, how much the customers loved him, how he fitted in so quickly after moving to Chester Falls, how creative he was—the list was endless. I started to think this Tom was so perfect he had to be a figment of their imagination.

What I hadn't counted on. What hadn't even crossed my mind, was that Tom might be around my age, and totally, unmistakably, my type.

One of the reasons I had never bothered coming out to my parents was that there had never been any boys at school that I'd been interested in. For the longest time I'd thought being bisexual was all in my mind because even though I found guys in magazines and on TV attractive, and had jerked off numerous times to images of these guys, in real life I'd never seen a guy I'd wanted to do those things with in Chester Falls.

And now, here he was, my unicorn, and he was very real, and very out of limits for more reasons than I wanted to list.

Initially I'd mistaken him for a customer. I mean, who

wears a bright-yellow sweater with rainbows to work? For a moment after we'd locked eyes it was as though time stopped; I wasn't sure what color his eyes were because they looked violet. Surely that wasn't a real eye color. His dark-brown hair had been styled to perfection.

When he'd come closer I'd frozen, but when my body had demanded I take a breath, my senses had been filled with the scent of perfection, home, and everything I'd always wanted.

After so many years of hiding, when I was put on the spot my instinct was to be the football player everyone knew, the icy-cold, hard-to-read person. I knew Tom would take it the wrong way, but it was safer that way. Better that he thinks I'm a jerk than to start looking at me like I'm not and then see more than I'm ready to show.

The customers by the checkout had been the perfect excuse to leave my mom to catch up with Tom. It had taken me a while to get my head around the new computer system they had, but I managed it, joking with the customers all the way.

After they'd left I didn't see my mom or Tom, so I'd gone back to the computer to study the new software. There was a tab with an icon I'd seen on the shopping bags but hadn't really noticed properly until now. I clicked on the tab and was shocked to see Mason's had its own website.

I was impressed by how professional the website looked. There were pages for the different departments, a home-styling option where customers could pick a few items they liked and the website gave them suggestions for other stuff that matched.

Tom came out from the storeroom carrying some throws. He winked as he walked past, sashaying down the aisle like he was on a catwalk. His pink jeans left nothing to the imagination. Tom had a good pair of legs and a great ass, and he knew it. Fuck. Me.

I took a deep breath and went back to learning the payment software, hoping boredom would deflate my half-hard cock before I went searching for my mom.

"Mom?"

"At the back, dear."

I saw my mom up a ladder trying to reach out for something on the top shelf right at the back of the storeroom. My heart was in my mouth as I picked up pace to hold the ladder in place for her.

"What are you looking for? Couldn't you have asked me to get it for you?"

"You were busy with those customers; besides, I've got it now."

She gave me a small box and then came down.

"This is where we keep the key to the safe. Last year when I hurt my back I got thinking what I would do if it had happened to your dad—"

"You hurt your back?" I interrupted. When had this happened? And why did I not know about it? My expression must have given away what I was thinking.

"It wasn't a big deal. I pulled a muscle and was out of action for a couple of weeks, nothing major. Anyway, your dad had to do everything for me but there was no issue with the store because he was the one that did all the paperwork. When I got back on my feet I made your dad write down all the information I'd need if he was ever sick."

"And it's all in the safe?"

"Yes, it's mainly passwords to access the checking accounts, but there's also the checkbook for the store account to pay some of the suppliers that still want to be paid that way.

Most of it is on automatic bill pay now. Anything you'll need is in there."

"Thanks, Mom, this will definitely make it easier."

Once my mom left to head back to the hospital I went to the office and got to work. I didn't know if there were any outstanding bills and didn't want my parents being chased for payments.

Hours later my head hurt from squinting and trying to understand my dad's handwriting to compare it to the information he had on spreadsheets on his computer. So far I had figured out there were no pending bills for this week, which was a bonus, but there was something else I couldn't make sense of.

I needed a coffee and fresh air. Instead of leaving through the back door I decided to go through the front and check in on Tom. We hadn't said much to each other earlier, well, I hadn't said much to him earlier, but I couldn't avoid him completely.

Tom didn't see me as I approached him. He was so focused on his notebook and whatever he was scribbling I couldn't help stop and look at him.

It was like I was looking at a different person. He wasn't trying to be anyone, or put up an image, which had clearly been what he'd been doing earlier on. His bottom lip was stuck between his teeth and occasionally his tongue came out at the same time as a tiny smile graced his lips.

He replaced his lip with his pen between his teeth and then looked up at the top of the window. He hummed an "ah-ha" as though he'd found the answer he was looking for. I thought I had time to make myself known, but in my trance, I forgot all it would take was a small turn and Tom would know I was there.

"Holy mother of Coco, are you trying to kill me?" He put his hands to his chest.

"Sorry, I didn't mean to frighten you."

"Then next time don't lurk like a creeper."

This guy was made of equal parts adorable and irritating, and I didn't know how to deal with it.

"I'm going to grab a coffee; can I get you one?"

"No, thank you," he said, going back to his notebook. I made my own mental note to ask my mom what it was Tom was working on.

With a large coffee and a slice of one of the cakes left for my parents in my stomach, I went back to the accounting. Tom had long shut the store and gone home by the time I figured out what it was I wasn't seeing earlier.

There was nothing wrong with my dad's records, there was nothing missing, or any mistakes with the invoices. They simply didn't have much money in the store account. My parents' business was surviving on a month-by-month basis.

I tried to get my head around my findings. They knew. There was no way they didn't know. Why hadn't they told me the business was struggling? My head was still spinning as I walked into the apartment after checking in on Troy, who had made his own dinner and was revising.

This wasn't the time to confront my parents about it. There was too much going on. But maybe I could figure out a way to help them? I didn't have much in terms of savings. After my retirement from football I'd used my savings to buy my apartment and now lived on my teacher's salary. I was also pretty sure they would refuse any kind of financial help, but maybe there was another way.

I smiled when I saw Aiden's name flash on my phone.

"Hey, Aid, what's up?"

"I'm the one who's meant to ask that." He laughed.

"My dad is okay. It was weird seeing him in the hospital, but I think he's coming home within the week."

I paused, debating if I should tell Aiden about Tom.

"Oh-huh, what's his name?"

Damn his perception.

"His name is Tom, and he's off-limits so this conversation ends here."

Aiden laughed. "I take it you haven't told your parents."

"It's one of the many reasons he's off-limits, and not even the most important one."

"Sounds complicated."

"Understatement of the year. It's late here so I'll catch you soon, okay?"

My knee hurt from the lack of movement so I decided on a hot shower before bed. I had a lot to do in the next three weeks, and my shattered knee and traitorous cock seemed hell-bent on making it hard for me. Pun intended.

TOM

$\mathscr{I}$’d never been one of those people that stay in bed on their day off. There was always too much to do to waste time in bed, especially when there’s no one else in it, but the fact I’d slept through my alarm and hadn’t woken up until ten in the morning was a testament to how tired I really was.

Between working extra hours in the store and then working at home too, I was beyond exhausted.

Or maybe it was because I hadn’t truly relaxed at work since Wren had arrived to help, even though he wasn’t helping at all. He spent the day in the office going through paperwork, or god knows what, and he only ever came out to give me a break so I wouldn’t have to eat my lunch behind the checkout desk.

I shouldn’t really complain about not spending more time with him in the store. The man was sex on legs, very shapely, thick legs that went on and on, ending in the best ass I’d ever seen. I was a bottom through and through; there was nothing I liked more than the feeling of a hard cock filling me up and hitting the right spot, but I was wondering if Wren's ass would make me change my mind.

"Get out of my head, you urghhh," I shouted as I pulled back the covers and got out of bed toward the bathroom.

"And you can go right down," I said to my dick. "You're no longer my friend, and if you don't stop with your stupid ideas about wanting the walking icicle I'll stop using the glitter soap you like."

I pondered over taking a cold shower, but I was determined to not let thoughts of Wren's ass, or his hard chest, change my morning routine and my super-hot shower.

Instead, I thought of my plans for the Pride window as I turned the water on and waited for it to be warm enough for me to step in the shower. I'd finally finished my plans and just needed to ask Troy if he could help me with some technical stuff before I showed it to Abi.

A rush of energy ran through me as I imagined bringing the window to life, placing furniture in the right place, the rug, fake fireplace, logs, and the photo frames and throw that would be the center pieces that held the scene together.

I stepped into the shower and let the warm water cascade over my skin, relaxing me.

As usual, my mind rarely obeyed my instructions and it started thinking about what Wren would think of my ideas for the window. Would he like it? Would he think it's too boring?

Wren never spent much time around me in the store. It had only been a few days and I could count on the fingers of my hand how many minutes we'd actually spent speaking to each other.

Did he think I was too much? And why the hell did I even care what he thought of me? For the love of fairy dust and all that glitters, Wren was a straight man who couldn't be less interested.

I put my frustration into picking the right outfit for today. As my idol said once, dress like you're going to meet your worst enemy. So, I did: tailored navy slacks, pink shirt, and navy vest, topped with a handkerchief popping out of the breast pocket.

"Wow, you're dressed to kill," Ben said when I walked into Bookmarked.

Ellie, his best friend and Charlie's sister-in-law, looked up from her book and whistled.

"Well, thanks." I did a full twirl, lifting a foot to show off the red sole of my shoe.

"Oh my god, are those...?" Ellie said in shock.

"They are indeed, my friend. They cost me a full month's salary a couple years ago but they're worth every cent."

Ben laughed. "Yeah, I have a book signed by A. Lawton that makes me feel the same way."

"A book cost you two grand?"

"Hell no, but something doesn't need to be expensive to make you feel good."

"So true. Coco said the best things in life are free, the second best are very expensive."

We left Ellie looking after Bookmarked and crossed the square toward Spilled Beans. I congratulated myself for only looking back once at my empty future store.

Indy wasn't behind the counter so we got a drink each and sat at one of the tables by the window facing the square.

"I'm going to enter the Pride bake-off," I said.

Ben snorted. "Are you serious? Do you know what happened last year?"

"Yeah, Indy told me."

I looked at the store across the square. "I haven't got the first clue about baking. If it was a sewing contest..."

"I'm sure you'd win hands down. Why do you want to

enter the bake-off?"

"The prize money. I have no clue if I have a chance in hell of winning, but by Coco and all that is shiny, if I win I can open my store."

I took a sip of my coffee, put the cup down, and set my notebook on the table.

"I need a plan...and a lot of bakeware."

"And a fire extinguisher," Indy said, joining us with his own cup of coffee in hand.

I threw him a deadly look I didn't mean and he laughed.

"Do you know what the challenges are yet?" Ben asked.

"No, but I figured I could practice anyway. I'm going to start easy and bake a cake."

Indy stopped halfway through sipping his coffee to laugh. "Easy? Man, you really have no idea, do you?"

"No." I stood up, curled my hand into a fist and bumped it against my chest. I looked up to the ceiling and proclaimed, "I haven't got a unicorn's ass clue about baking, but I'll be damned if I'm not going to win this competition."

In my self-absorbed state of mind, I'd forgotten there were a handful of people in the coffee shop, who all cheered at my declaration.

I plopped back down on my chair and called out to Indy's barista, "Jake, can I get a rainbow cupcake with extra sprinkles please? I need to recharge my superpowers."

After serving his customers, Jake placed the cupcake and a fresh cup of coffee in front of me. I ran my finger through the icing and licked it clean, the smooth sweet taste of the buttercream giving me instant happiness.

"I hear Wren is back," Ben said.

"Yeah, he's been coming by for coffee almost every day," Indy said.

Ignoring their comments, I put a fork through the

cupcake, cutting it in half and filling my mouth with the soft vanilla sponge.

"I think I'm going to make a vanilla cake and fill it with buttercream," I said. "I found this recipe online; it looks pretty simple. I just need to get the ingredients and a baking pan."

When I looked up from the crumbs of my cupcake both Indy and Ben were staring at me.

"What?"

They looked at each other and then Ben leaned across to put his hand on my forehead.

"Temperature seems fine. How's the pulse?" he asked and Indy pressed his fingers on the inside of my wrist and pretended to look at his non-existent watch.

"A little faster than normal, but nothing to be concerned about."

I rolled my eyes and put my notebook back in my bag, readying myself to leave. I had groceries to buy, and a baking pan that I knew I'd only get in one place in Chester Falls.

"Sounds like someone is avoiding a certain topic of conversation," Ben said.

"Would it be the same someone who currently works for said topic of conversation?" Indy replied.

I sat back on my chair and pretended to pick a piece of lint off my vest.

"You two clearly think you're onto something here, so why don't you spit it out so we can all carry on with our day?" I said as nonchalantly as I could.

My two friends shared another look but it was Ben that spoke.

"So, how long have you been attracted to Wren? And I'm not accepting anything less than the day you met."

I sent Indy a pleading look but it seemed I was outnumbered. What could I tell them? That yes, I was super attracted to a guy who I'd barely had a conversation with, who was undoubtedly straight, and even if he wasn't he'd be off-limits on account of being my boss.

In the past I'd never had to rein in my attraction to a man, but now more than ever I couldn't afford to lose my job. In Boston I could go to any upmarket store and get a job on the back of my career with Clarence's. In Chester Falls there not only weren't as many well-paid jobs but if I caused trouble for the Masons no doubt I'd find it extra hard to get a new job.

So, no. There was no point going there and thinking about Wren in any kind of way other than a boss slash work colleague.

The dinging bell on the door saved me from replying to Ben's question because his gaze zeroed in on Tristan who was coming in. The connection between them was so special I felt like an intruder watching them as Tristan approached and stole a kiss before he sat next to Ben.

"Anyone been to Mason's recently? Who's the hot guy?" Tristan asked.

Ben elbowed him, which made me chuckle because he didn't even look mad at the comment.

"Baby, you know I'm all yours," Tristan said, pulling Ben closer.

"I know." Ben whispered something in Tristan's ear and I saw him adjusting in his seat. God, when was the last time I'd had that kind of intimacy with someone else? Joked, teased? Had I ever had it?

"That's Wren," Indy said. "He's Jonas and Abi's eldest son. He lives in California, but I guess he came back because of Jonas."

"Anyone care about my cake?" I asked, letting some of my frustration show, and hoping they'd think it was baking related rather than Wren related.

"I'll help you with whatever you need, but first you have to answer Ben's question," Indy said.

I huffed and they both shrugged. Tristan looked confused.

"Fine, I confess, he's attractive."

Indy gestured for me to carry on.

"I'm going to need another cupcake and a free coffee," I demanded, and it took a whole ten seconds for both to appear in front of me. I'd need to be careful around Jake because he had the hearing of a moth, it seemed.

"Okay, okay, I'm attracted to Wren. I mean, who wouldn't? Have you seen the guy? He's like a Ralph Lauren walking advert. But it doesn't matter because he's straight and he's my bosses' son. Also, he can't stand me so there's that too. Can we go back to more important issues, like how am I going to win the bake-off?"

None of them argued with my reasoning so I accepted that they agreed with me. Good.

I realized then that it was possible that both Ben and Indy had attended the same school as Wren. I wondered if he'd been as closed off and quiet as a teenager as he seemed now. One thing I would have bet my mom's pearls on, and that was how gorgeous he would have been back then.

He was a football player, according to Abi, so I bet he had all the girls hanging from his arms begging for attention, and the gay kids watching from afar, feeling jealous they didn't stand a chance.

I shook my errant thoughts off and opened my notebook again to show Indy my shopping list. He looked at it and added some items I didn't have on there, such as parchment paper and a hand mixer. Yep, I needed to go to Mason's because there was no way the grocery store would have the mixer.

WREN

The first thought I had when I woke up was that Tom was off work today. As I lay in bed, the sun rising slowly outside, I ignored the need to touch my aching morning wood.

What I couldn't ignore was the feeling in my chest when I thought of spending the day on my own at the store. It was probably natural that after so many years away I was apprehensive about being in the store on my own. After all, there would be no one to answer those questions I used to know the answers to.

Despite only working in the store just over a month, Tom seemed to know everything and everyone. He knew the regular customers, what they liked, where everything was in the storeroom, and he seemed to thrive on finding the one item customers didn't know they needed until Tom told them about it.

He was a good salesman, but he also cared about the people. That much was evidenced by the people that seemed to come in just to greet him almost on a daily basis.

Yesterday I'd caught myself watching him from afar as he'd

given a guy advice on what to wear for a job interview. He'd asked questions about what kind of job it was and who he'd been working for, and then he'd offered advice for the interview itself.

"Remember, they are the ones with the problem. They need someone to do the job. You're interviewing them, not the other way round. They have more to lose by picking the wrong person. Your only job is to show them you're the right one," he'd said to the guy, who couldn't have been more than twenty years old but looked like he desperately needed the opportunity from his focus as he'd hung on Tom's every single word.

I too had been hung on Tom, but not just his words. I'd been hung on the way his hands moved when he talked as thought they were an extension of his words, the way his clothes fitted him perfectly in a style that was so much Tom I was not sure there would have been another person in the world that would pull it off so effortlessly.

I'd been so distracted that I hadn't reacted fast enough when the conversation between Tom and the guy had ended. Tom's eyes had caught mine from behind the shelves and he'd stopped, plastering a smile on his face as the guy had thanked him for his help and left the store.

He'd looked down for a moment, but when he'd looked back up at me he'd said the guy needed help and couldn't afford to buy anything from us. Then he'd left toward the storeroom, coming out a little while later with a basket full of notebooks, pens, and other stuff for the stationery shelf.

He'd had his usual defiant look on but there was also something else. He cared about Mason's, and I'd bet he felt bad that he hadn't got a sale from the customer, but at the same time I'd seen how he'd spoken to the customer, which showed a side of Tom I hadn't met. I'd wanted to tell him that it hadn't mattered, and that if the guy got the job he'd likely come back to the store and buy something for himself with the paycheck, but that would also have meant admitting I'd pretty much witnessed the whole conversation.

I pulled the covers off me and got up in frustration. Normally I'd go out for a run, but my knee was still giving me some trouble and I didn't want to push it. It was early enough so I decided to go over to my parents' and have breakfast with Troy before heading to the store. I just needed to get rid of this stupid erection first.

In the week since I'd been home I'd done nothing else but work in the store and the occasional trip to the hospital to see my dad.

Well, that wasn't entirely true, I'd done plenty of thinking about Tom. Even now, despite having some paperwork to go through while there were no customers in the store, I was staring at the boxes that Tom had lined up neatly behind the counter in preparation for the Pride window.

Curiosity got the best of me and I opened one of them. I expected to see nothing but rainbows, glitter, and color. Instead what I found was a number of household items that you wouldn't really associate with Pride.

Our window displays had won in the past because we'd gone all out with the color, showing that Mason's was proud to support our LGBTQ community.

Little did my parents know we were very much part of that community. I'd decided a few days ago I would tell my parents the truth. Sure, they'd probably be a little disappointed, but I didn't have any doubt they'd understand and support me fully.

Still, the lack of color worried me. Mason's hadn't won the window competition in a few years and there was something about me being home and coming out to my parents that felt that winning the competition would be the cherry on top.

I'd need to speak to Tom tomorrow about his plans for the window.

My cellphone dinged under the counter. I pulled it out and saw a text had come through from one of my school buddies, Connor.

Connor: A bird told me my man Wren was home from California, but that couldn't possibly be true because I'm sure he would have told me.

I smiled at the screen. Connor and I had been on the football team in high school, and even though he hadn't wanted to pursue a career in sports, he just loved being active so much we'd spent a lot of time training together off the field.

Wren: Would that bird have blue hair by any chance?

Connor: I'm not confirming or denying.

Wren: I was just about to text you anyway. You up for a drink at the Falls tonight?

Connor: Sure. You mind if I bring a friend?

Wren: The more the merrier. I'm in the mood for one of their sugary cocktails.

The next text was a thumbs up emoji, so I put the phone down. We'd had a small delivery of scented candles this morning so I decided to work on that.

Putting the candles out was a good distraction. Even though it was a mindless task of opening boxes, lining up the candles on the shelf, and breaking the boxes down, it was good to move around. I liked being productive and without the chance to go running this was as close to exercise as I could get.

I looked to the front door when I heard the bell and saw Tom coming in. My stomach did a little flip.

He looked around and I thought I saw a flicker of disappointment when he didn't see me right away.

"Hey," I said.

"Oh hi, I thought Troy was helping out today."

Okay, so he wasn't looking for me then.

"He's coming after school."

Tom's violet eyes looked a little more blue today, probably because of the clothes he wore. I'd noticed that depending on what he wore, his eyes almost changed color to match. I smiled at the thought that even Tom's eyes had their own sense of fashion, which didn't surprise me in the least considering who they belonged to.

"Here." He raised a cup of coffee from Spilled Beans in my direction. Jesus, how long had I been staring at him?

"Oh, you... you got me coffee?"

"Um, yeah I noticed you like the same coffee I do and I was already on my way here to buy a few things so I thought I'd bring you coffee. Anyway, I know what I want and where it is so..."

As soon as I took the coffee from him he walked around me and left me standing there, thinking about the fact that he knew how I took my coffee even though I'd never told him, and how I'd felt a little spark when our fingers touched.

I put the coffee down on the counter and went after Tom.

"Thank you for the coffee," I said.

"You're welcome. It was Indy's idea."

"But you said—"

"Do you know where I can find parchment paper? It's the only thing on my list that we don't seem to have here."

I wasn't sure why he'd changed his story but it didn't surprise me. Tom seemed to run hot and cold with me all the time. It was confusing, and I had no clue how to figure him out, so I decided to get onto a safer topic.

"I know you're off work today, so I'm sorry for asking, but the Pride window stuff."

"What about it?"

"I've opened some boxes and, well, there's nothing colorful in them at all. Won't the window be a bit boring?"

I saw him grip the shopping basket so tight his knuckles were white. He looked around to see if there was anyone else in the store and then came so close to me I could smell his sweet flowery scent.

My stomach clenched with want and I had to bite the inside of my cheek to stop myself from letting out a moan that would give away how my body was reacting to Tom's proximity.

"Do you wear a lot of color, Wren?"

"What?"

Like the day we'd met, Tom raised his hand, but this time I didn't stop him. He traced the outline of my shirt collar, all the way down to the buttons. He played with the top one and spoke again.

"Do you wear a lot of color?"

"No, I guess I don't, but why—" He put his finger on my lips to stop me from talking.

"Do you think you're boring?"

He removed his finger and went back to the button, twisting it like he was about to pop it out and open my shirt. I swallowed before I replied.

"I...no. I guess I'm normal, I don't know."

His eyes never left mine, which was a good thing, because if he stepped back there was not a chance he wouldn't see the outline of my fully hard cock through my jeans.

"Normal. That's an interesting word," he said, removing his hand to support the other holding the basket. "I guess you wouldn't know what it's like to be LGBT. We come in all colors, shapes, and sizes. While we should all be proud of who we are, sometimes it's okay to want to blend in, be a regular person. Sometimes we want to go home to our plain home that is just cozy, when the rest of our lives are so loud and colorful and full of fight."

He then walked to the checkout desk, saying, "Can you ring my stuff, please?"

"Sure."

I thought about what he'd said and it made sense to me. My mom had trusted Tom so I should too.

He was on his way out when I called to him.

"Tom." He turned, his hand on the door handle, ready to go. "Like you said, we come in all colors, shapes, and sizes."

His eyes widened but he didn't say anything before he turned the handle and left the store.

I stood there staring at the closed door, unsure of what to do.

A customer came in and behind them a small gust of wind blew a leaflet inside the store. I picked it up before a customer stepped on it and slipped. When I turned it over, the words *Ten Thousand Dollars Could Be Yours* caught my attention.

TOM

I ran to the oven as soon as the timer went off. This was my third batch of cake and so far none had worked and I had no clue why.

The first batch was nearly burned on the outside and totally raw on the inside. I'd figured it was the temperature of the oven, so I'd fixed that on the second batch, but that one had sunk in the middle.

Through the oven door the cake looked okay, but I was scared of opening it in case it was another ruined attempt.

I'd never had any assumptions that this would be an easy challenge, but I'd followed all the instructions on the recipe. How was it going so wrong?

"For the love of Cinderella's fairy godmothers, please be a good one," I said, talking to the cake like it could understand me.

My cellphone rang but I had to ignore it.

"Come to momma," I said, opening the oven door. I touched the top of the cake and it felt bouncy and hard enough that it shouldn't be raw. "Oh yes, baby, you're looking fine. Now let's get you all cooled down."

I set the cake, still inside the tin, on top of the stove and admired it for a moment. There was a nice dome in the middle of the cake and the smell of vanilla all over the apartment gave me a happy buzz. Maybe I could do this, after all.

My cellphone rang again and I saw Indy's name flash on the screen.

"Hey."

"Oh my god, Tom, I was about to call the fire department."

"Why?"

"Patty Sims came in complaining about someone setting off their fire alarm all afternoon and I know she lives near you."

"Oh that. Yeah, things were tricky to start with but I have a super-adorable cake cooling now. It's so adorable I'm not sure I'll be able to eat it."

Indy laughed.

"Are you feeling a little bit more confident about the competition?"

I snorted. "Have you seen the list of challenges? I've been baking all afternoon and all I have to show for it is two ruined cakes and one *maybe* okay cake."

"I'm off tonight so we can swap skills if you want. Pastry for cocktails."

"Sounds wonderful, but Connor wants to take me to the Falls for a drink. I'm pretty sure Charlie is behind the idea. He made me promise to not stay at home every night watching fashion documentaries and making clothes."

"Well, a promise is a promise. Besides, Connor is nice, you'll have a good time."

I sighed. "Yeah, I know. Why don't you join us?"

"Only if you buy me a cocktail."

"Got it."

After I got off the phone I checked on the cake, and it was still warm so I got in the shower to get ready for Connor to pick me up.

Charlie was absolutely right, outside of work I was a homebody and it was good for me to meet new people. I'd been lucky to already know Indy when I moved to Chester Falls and then met Ben and Tristan, but I needed to get out of my comfort zone. Who knew, maybe I'd even find someone who was totally gay and totally up for some fun.

After my shower I wrapped the cake in plastic wrap, ready to try my hand at buttercream icing tomorrow, and went back to my bedroom to get dressed.

Normally I'd spend hours thinking about what to wear, even if it was just for a few cocktails out with friends, but today I wasn't quite in the mood. I decided to go with a simple pairing of classic jeans, white T-shirt, and a jacket.

I looked at myself in the mirror and almost didn't recognize the person in front of me. Connor was due to pick me up shortly but I still had time for a short phone call to one of my favorite people.

"Tom, sweetie, how are you?"

"Hey, Gina."

"Oh no, what's up?"

I looked at the phone to double check I wasn't on a video call. The woman was too damned perceptive.

Gina was Charlie and Connor's aunt and the sweetest wildcat you could ever meet. She was also totally in love with my cocktails and she loved shopping, which made us a pairing made in Coco heaven.

"I'm wearing sneakers. I don't know what's wrong with me."

"Tom Jones, there is nothing wrong with you, but sneakers? You need CRP."

"Don't you mean CPR?"

"CRP. Cocktail Rehabilitation Program. Or maybe some retail therapy?"

I laughed.

"Gina, I can't afford to shop now. But I'm having some CRP with Connor tonight at the Falls."

"Good. Connor isn't the best person to lead you astray, but I'm sure you can do that all on your own."

"Thanks, G. Not really in the mood to be led astray, but who knows what'll happen at pumpkin hour," I said.

"I'll see you soon, then, sweetie."

Listening to Gina's voice cheered me up instantly, and I made a note in my calendar to arrange a cocktail evening for us. I wanted her to try my Minty Librarian Delight and the Pure Boogie Sunset.

The Falls wasn't as packed as I'd seen it previously, which I guessed was because there wasn't a live band on today. Connor spotted an empty table immediately so we sat down to claim our spot.

I'd been to the Falls a few times before with Charlie. It was a charming bar with great drinks, nice music, and the people were super friendly.

"Look, Brent is here today, let me say hi to him. Can I get you a drink while I'm at the bar?" I asked Connor after I saw my favorite barman was on duty tonight.

"Thanks, man, a beer would be great."

I sat on a stool at the bar while I waited for my turn. Brent looked like an artist when he made his cocktails and I loved watching him.

When he saw me he winked and I blew him a kiss. I knew he didn't mean anything by it, but I didn't miss the look that the guy who sat on the opposite side of the bar sent my way.

"Hey, gorgeous, what can I get you today?"

"Do your worst, and a beer for Connor please," I said.

Brent never took his eyes off the crowd at the bar when he was preparing his drinks, it was a minor miracle he never spilled a drop or broke a glass.

"Who's the guy who's looking at you like you're his property?"

Brent looked over his shoulder and I saw a blush rising in his cheeks.

"Oh, no, he's just a friend. Actually, he's my sister's ex. After they broke up he went traveling for a few months and now he's back."

I stood up on my stool and hooked my finger to get Brent to come closer. He did, and as I whispered in his ear, "I think I know why he's your sister's ex," I had my suspicions semi-confirmed when the guy downed his beer and left.

Brent looked confused, and when he saw the guy was no longer there the disappointment in his eyes was clear.

I went back to my table and nearly dropped my cocktail when I saw who was sitting with Connor.

"Wren."

He looked up from the table and seemed as surprised to see me.

"Tom."

"You know each other?" Connor asked, looking at us. "Oh, of course you do. Sorry, I forgot Tom works at Mason's."

Wren scooted over on the bench to make room for me so I sat next to him. Connor grabbed the beer from me and took a swig.

"Sorry, I didn't know you were coming so I didn't get you a drink," I said to Wren.

He smiled. I didn't know how it was possible that his eyes still looked so bright and blue even in the dark lighting of the bar.

I forced myself to look away and focused on Connor instead.

"So, did you go to school together or something?"

Connor smiled and raised his beer. "Yeah, me and my man here were in the football team. He was the quarterback and I was a wide receiver. We were the best."

"That we were," Wren said.

"Do you remember that time we played against Seymour High?"

"How could I not? It was the game that got me my college scholarship."

"How's it going for you over in San Diego? You still playing? I probably should pay more attention to the leagues but, fuck, work keeps me so busy these days I can't even keep up with myself."

"Are you still in that place you went to after college?" Wren asked.

"No, I'm now doing HR project management for a construction company in New Haven. Pay is good, hours are shit, and most days I'm not sure if I want to kill the team or myself."

"Shit, man, that sounds awful."

Connor shrugged, finished his beer, and stood up. "Going for seconds, can I get you one?" he asked Wren.

"A soda would be great, thanks. Got an early day tomorrow."

Connor looked at me, but I hadn't touched my drink so he went over to the bar.

"You're not working tomorrow," I said.

"I know, but he doesn't know that, and I don't want him driving if he has more than one beer."

"Thank you."

His smile did something to my insides. Why did he have to be so fucking beautiful?

"Why did you avoid the football question?" I asked.

"What?"

"Connor asked you about your career and you avoided the question."

"No I didn't, I just decided to catch up on my friend's life rather than talk about mine."

His voice was even and his reply measured, but I'd been sitting next to him for a while. I'd been more aware of how he moved, breathed, and relaxed as he talked to Connor than I'd been of my own drink, and that was saying a lot because Brent's cocktails were the best.

As soon as Connor had brought up the topic of football Wren had tensed up. It wasn't my place to push, I'd only been curious about his life in California, but we weren't friends or anything, so I kept further questions to myself. Hell, as it was we barely spoke to each other on account that most of the time he was like an ice box. Tonight was the first time I'd seen him relax a little.

"Why do you keep checking your phone?" Wren asked. "Are you waiting for a call or something?"

"Indy said he'd come tonight."

Wren nodded as he stared at me for a moment before he looked away.

Just then my phone buzzed with a message from Indy.

Indy: *Sorry, babe. I've had a better offer tonight. Say hi to Connor for me.*

Tom: **gasps**

Indy: *I'll tell you all about it tomorrow.*

Tom: *I wouldn't expect anything less. Don't do anything I wouldn't do!*

We stayed at the bar for another hour, during which

Connor had two more beers while I changed to soda after finishing my cocktail.

Wren insisted on following us as I drove Connor's car to his place and then he gave me a lift home.

"How's your dad? Is he coming home soon?" I asked, needing to fill the silence in the car.

"He's doing well. Coming home in a few days."

I looked at Wren and even in the darkness I saw him smile.

"What's up?" I asked.

We stopped at a red light and he looked at me.

"Why did you move to Chester Falls?"

I wasn't sure how to answer his question. The truth was that I didn't want to be alone in Boston, but I didn't want to sound like a sad little puppy.

"Sorry, I shouldn't pry." He looked forward just as the light turned green, and we were on the move again.

"No, it sounds silly, but without Charlie in Boston I didn't feel like I was home anymore. I already knew some people here, and if I'm here I'll see him when he comes home too. Besides..."

"Besides what?"

I looked out of the window into the dark night. Unlike the city, Chester Falls was mostly dark at night. I kinda liked it. It was peaceful.

"Nothing, never mind."

"Okay."

I didn't expect Wren to come out of the car and walk me to the door of my apartment building, but that's what he did.

"Um, thank you for driving me home. I'd have taken a cab from Connor's but it was nice not having to," I said, becoming very aware that how he stood in front of me looked very much like the end of a date.

Stop it, Tom. This is not a date. Wren is straight.

"Just wanted to make sure you're home safe."

He didn't move, and I didn't know what to do. His eyes were fixed on my mouth, and I instinctively wet my lips.

A shiver of anticipation ran down my spine.

"Wren, what did you mean earlier?"

He looked up to meet my eyes.

"When?"

"When you said *we* come in all colors, shapes, and sizes? Did you mean—"

"I've got to go." His sudden change almost gave me whiplash. "I'll stop by tomorrow to cover your lunch."

I didn't have time to process anything before I was left standing alone, wondering if there was more to Wren than my initial assessment.

WREN

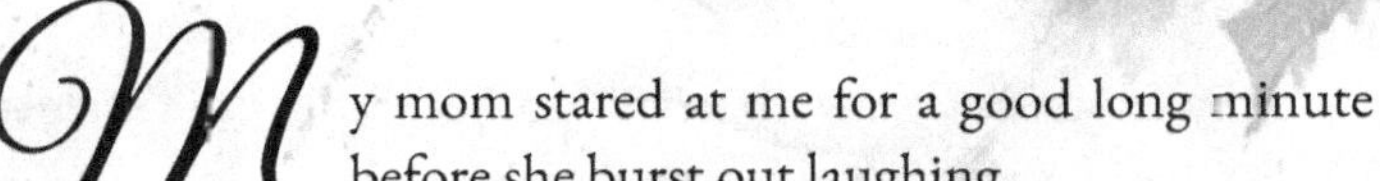

My mom stared at me for a good long minute before she burst out laughing.

"What's going on?" Troy asked, coming into the kitchen where I sat with a cup of coffee, and my own mother laughing in my face after I told her about the Pride bake-off.

"Mom's being a real adult about...something." Well, if this was the reception I got from my own mom, maybe I should just keep it to myself.

We'd received notification yesterday from the hospital that my dad was being discharged today, so, to make everything easier, Mom had decided to keep the store closed for the day.

It hadn't taken long to go through the care plan for my dad. We had the right medication, a list of recommendations, and a follow-up appointment booked.

With Dad resting in bed after the car journey, Mom had retreated to the kitchen to make sure we didn't have anything in the house Dad wasn't allowed to have, and that had included raiding all his jelly bean hiding places. I'd almost felt sorry for him until I realized just exactly how many there were.

I'd used the opportunity of having my mom's undivided

attention to ask her for help with the bake-off, something I was now regretting.

"Come on, honey. You just threw me off. You were never interested in it before."

"People! Is someone going to enlighten the teenager here?" Troy said, taking a cookie from the jar and sitting at the table.

"I'm entering the Pride bake-off."

To his credit, Troy didn't laugh. "Dude, do you know what happens at these things?"

"Yes, yes someone got their hair on fire last year." I took a sip of my coffee and put the mug back down. Troy's eyebrows were raised. "What? Come on, it's baking, how dangerous can it be?"

Troy snorted. "Bro, two years ago Mr. Stone, the science teacher, gave all the judges food poisoning."

"I take it he didn't win," I said deadpan.

"Oh no, he won alright. After they had to delay the competition until the judges were okay again everyone donated the money he was trying to raise for the school lab. There was so much, we even got new computers for the school."

I got up and put my arms around my mom from behind, kissing her head and rocking us sideways.

"You don't play fair. You know I'm powerless to my son's bear hugs," she said.

"Don't know what you're talking about, I just missed you and wanted to give you a hug, but if this is the reception my hugs get then maybe I'll keep them to myself."

She put an arm over mine, tightening our embrace, and I fist-pumped Troy in victory.

I spent the next couple of hours learning all about the ratio of butter to flour to sugar and how to make a creamy batter that would rise evenly.

Half of it I wouldn't have ever understood if we weren't doing it at the same time, but when the cake came out of the oven a perfect color and smelling delicious I couldn't stop smiling.

Even Dad had come down from the bedroom at some point to observe what was going on.

Making buttercream was another challenge, especially when I added too much powdered sugar to the butter and ended up surrounded by a sweet white powder cloud.

Dad left us again, claiming that breathing sugar wasn't allowed on his new post-operation diet, and Troy joined him, likely because he didn't want to be drafted for clean-up duties.

With the cake nearly cool and the buttercream done I started washing up the cake tin and all the utensils. I didn't remember my mom ever having this much to clean up whenever she'd made cakes before.

"So, are you going to tell me why you're entering the competition?" my mom asked.

She had a knowing smile on her face. One I couldn't understand.

"Mom, have you seen the stores accounts lately?"

Her smile left her lips, but she didn't seem mad that I'd brought the topic up.

"I know, Wren. Things have been hard and we've prioritized expenses we feel are essential, but we're still in the black."

"Yes, Mom, but for how long? All you need is something going wrong with the store and you'll have a bill you can't afford to pay."

She put her hand on my arm and squeezed. "Sweetheart, I don't want you to worry about it. Everything is in hand. I am so happy you are here though, we all missed you."

A pang of guilt hit me. I rubbed my knee and wondered if it would be so bad to tell my parents about my injury.

I'd noticed that around the house there were still photos of me with various sporting medals and with the football team in our Chester High kit, but the medals themselves as well as the cups were no longer on top of the kitchen cupboards or on the hallway sideboard.

Instead of feeling sad that my parents had moved on from worshiping the victories of their teenage son, I felt relieved that they had. I'd always known they only cared for football because I did. They hadn't missed a game, even when they'd had to take it in turns to attend with the other looking after Troy, and they'd talked the ear off anyone who'd brought the topic up in the store.

I opened my mouth to ask my mom about the medals and trophies but she spoke instead.

"Come on, let's ice this cake. I could do with a slice and a cup of tea."

"Yes, ma'am."

"Oh, and, honey? I think this competition is just what you need."

I narrowed my eyes as her knowing smile returned.

It was strange being back at my old high school, not to mention that I'd never in a million years imagined I'd be back there, especially not to participate in a baking competition. It was bittersweet because while I had great memories of all the achievements, friendships, and even to a certain degree the classes, there was part of me that always felt like it wasn't complete.

I hadn't knowingly hidden my bisexuality, but I certainly had ignored it to a level where I hadn't even been sure I was bisexual at all. I'd put it down to spending so much time with guys on the football field, locker rooms, and even hanging out as friends, rather than genuine attraction to the same gender.

The sports hall hadn't changed one bit. The bleachers were slowly filling up with people on both sides of the court. Some were holding up signs and cheering for people I didn't know.

An unsuspecting visitor would easily assume everyone was here for a basketball game, but today at the center of the court there wasn't a team, a group of cheerleaders, or a mascot. Instead, a row of tables covered in white cloths occupied the center of the court. Some had cake boxes lined up in front of little cards.

"Excuse me," I said to a woman I saw holding a clipboard.

"Oh hi, you must be one of the contestants. Pick a random spot on the tables and place your cake with the box lid covering it. Write your name on the card in front of the cake and face it down."

"Thank you."

Everyone seemed to have placed the cakes in order from left to right, so I went to the nearest empty card and put my cake down as the woman had explained. All the other cakes were covered, so I had no idea what my competition looked like. I also didn't know who the other contestants were.

With so many random groups of people hovering on the sides of the court, it was hard to know who was a contestant and who was supporting.

I picked a seat on the front row and took my cellphone out.

Wren: Would you believe me if I told you I'm back in high school?

*Aiden: *shudders**

Wren: You didn't like high school then?

Aiden: I didn't go to high school. I went to a private school, but it's not a memory I want to revisit. What are you doing at school anyway? I thought you passed your reading test years ago.

Wren: Funny. I entered a baking contest.

Aiden: You don't need to be embarrassed about your literacy shortcomings. I love you despite of them.

Wren: Thanks Nora Roberts. And I'm serious, fuck you very much.

Aiden followed with a shocked woman GIF that made me laugh aloud.

"Wren?"

I looked up to see Tom standing in front of me looking every bit the sexiest man I'd ever seen in my life.

He had a burgundy three-piece suit on that fitted him like it had been sewn directly onto his frame. Unlike the other night when he'd worn what could have been considered normal plain clothing, today he was more like what I expected from him.

Not that he hadn't looked sexy as fuck in just jeans and a white shirt, but there was something more in his eyes when he dressed up.

I gestured for him to take a seat next to me. He moved slowly as though he was reluctant to do it but then relented.

All the cards on the tables now had a cake behind them and the lady with the clipboard was going around the room asking people to take a seat.

"You're here reliving high school memories?" Tom asked.

I chuckled. "Not quite."

"Supporting a contestant you know?"

"Not that either."

Tom's brows furrowed and for a moment I got lost in his eyes until I remembered he was waiting for my real reason for being here.

"I erm, entered the bake-off," I said, rubbing the back of my neck.

"What?"

A few people turned their heads when Tom's shriek was heard over the quieting hall. He looked upset, no, angry.

I pointed at the tables. "I'm one of the contestants. What are you doing here? Do you know someone entering?"

"No, I'm one of the contestants too."

I should have been upset that we were competing against each other, but Tom's cute pout made it hard.

I chuckled. "Looks like we're rivals then."

"Looks like we are," he said, crossing his arms and facing forward.

Benny and Momma Ruth from Benny's Diner were two of the judges, who were now removing the box lids and revealing the cakes underneath. I didn't recognize the other two.

A tall well-built man wearing a dark-gray suit walked into the hall as soon as all the cakes were on display. He was holding a microphone.

"Welcome. It is my pleasure as the mayor of Chester Falls to kick off our yearly Pride festival by welcoming all the contestants of our most popular event: the Pride bake-off."

Everyone cheered. The mayor put his hands up to ask for silence.

"Now, we know why this is the more popular event, but I'd like to keep the town's liability insurance cost down, so please all be safe and enjoy the festival. I will now hand over to the judges who are testing these wonderful cakes blind to pick the six contestants who will go to the live rounds."

It took a good hour until the judges had tasted and scored all the cakes. Every time they'd moved on to a new one someone in the crowd had shouted out their support for the contestant.

From where we sat all the cakes looked pretty much the same. The brief was to make a chocolate fudge cake, and all the cakes looked fudgy to me.

"This is great, just great," I heard Tom muttering under his breath.

What was his problem?

"Looks like they're ready to announce who goes to the next round," I said.

Tom replied with a huff.

I looked at him, trying not to laugh. "Are you going to set me on fire?"

"I'm making no promises."

TOM

I couldn't believe what had just happened. I balled my fists and walked out of the hall as soon as the judges had announced the six contestants that would go through to the live rounds.

The two miles from the high school grounds to the town center weren't enough to walk off my anger, but I wasn't thinking clearly anyway so by the time I walked into Spilled Beans I wasn't just fuming.

I was close to tears and even angrier with myself for feeling this way.

"I'm going to fucking kill him. How dare he? How is he even allowed?"

I paced the length of the coffee shop, feeling like a ball of nerves ready to explode.

Indy stepped in front of me by the door and put his hands on both my shoulders to stop me.

"What's the matter?" he asked. His indigo-colored hair looked bluer in the light than when he was behind the counter.

I looked around and saw an old lady get up and pick up her handbag to leave.

"Fuck, shit I'm so sorry. I'm just so... I didn't even see if you had any customers."

"Don't worry about it. Mrs. Donner had been nursing the same empty cup of coffee she ordered three hours ago while she read the free paper, so I've not lost any business with your dramatic entrance."

Indy's dark-blue eyes searched my face for some kind of answer for my current state.

"What's the matter? Did you not..."

I shook my head. "It's not that."

"You mean you went through to the next round?"

He beamed at me and I couldn't help reacting. I'd run out of the hall so quickly I hadn't given myself the chance to celebrate.

"I'm shocked you'd think I didn't," I teased. After my vanilla cake attempt I'd decided to practice under Indy's supervision, and he'd spent the last couple of nights watching me as I'd tried to perfect a chocolate fudge cake recipe I'd found online.

"If you'd seen your face when you walked in you'd understand. So what's made you so angry then?"

"Wren is in the bake-off too."

I didn't know what kind of reaction I was expecting from Indy, but no reaction was not it.

"You knew?"

Indy grabbed my arm and led me to a table.

"Do you want coffee or something stronger?"

"Both. And it's going to be on the house."

He laughed but went behind the counter. A minute later he placed a black coffee and a marshmallow-filled cupcake in front of me.

"Extra reinforcement," he clarified.

"You mean apology."

He shrugged. "Cupcake, muffin. All cake."

"I don't understand what he's doing there."

"It's a public competition, Tom."

"I know, but why him? Isn't it enough that he's in the store all day, and now he's part of this too? I mean... I..."

Indy held my hands and brought them up to his mouth and placed a kiss on my knuckles.

"Sweetie, can I ask you a question?"

My hands felt a little clammy in his.

"Do you have feelings for Wren?"

He looked so concerned I couldn't not tell him the truth.

"I don't have feelings per se. It's more that my heart rate increases when he's nearby, and my eyes have this nasty habit of following his ass every time he walks away from me. Then there's his stupid blue eyes. I mean, who has eyes like that? They're like a swimming pool on a summer day. Yesterday he unwrapped all the snow globes for me so I could put them on the shelf... I don't like Bubble Wrap..." In my thinking about Wren I almost forgot I was speaking to Indy.

"So, no feelings, huh?"

"None whatsoever." I grinned. "Anyway, it doesn't matter since he's straight. And now he's my enemy too."

Indy raised his eyebrows. "Look, it's not my place to say this, but I don't think everything is as it seems with Wren. Maybe get to know him a little better and you might find that you're more compatible than you think."

Did Indy mean what I thought he meant? No one had openly commented on Wren's sexuality, his parents included, and I'd made my assumptions. Then there was the comment he'd made and then avoided when I'd asked him about it.

"It doesn't matter," I said, standing up as a customer came

into the coffee shop. "I need to see Tristan about the next challenge so I've got to go. Thanks for letting me barge in and behave like a crazy person, and thanks for calming me down."

Indy hugged me. "Anytime, gorgeous."

I crossed the square, praying Tristan was at Bookmarked. My heart jumped for joy when I saw his car parked on the spot around the side of the bookstore.

"Hi, Ellie, is Tristan here?" I said.

"Tom! Hannah and I were talking the other day, you need to come over for dinner soon. We miss you."

"You both miss my cocktails."

"That too." She giggled.

Ellie and Hannah, who was Charlie's and Connor's sister, had been married nearly a year. It was during the events of their wedding that Charlie and Kris had met and got together.

"You'll need to take a ticket and join the line."

"Damn Gina," Ellie said pouting.

I chuckled.

"Oh, you wanted Tristan. He's in the storeroom with Ben having sex."

"Jesus Christ, Ellie," Ben said. "How many times do I need to tell you we're not having sex every time we're upstairs."

Ben stood by the door leading to the storeroom, his hands on his hips. Tristan a little taller behind Ben with a grin on his face, nodding. Ben elbowed him.

"Babe!"

"I'm gonna need to move to a new town where there aren't so many happy couples. It's hard to be grumpy and miserable when everyone is so happy," I said.

"Tom, you'll find your guy," Tristan said, looking at Ben, "and sometimes he finds you instead." He wrapped his arms around Ben who literally melted into Tristan's embrace. Okay, maybe not literally.

"Ugh, stop it. Tristan, I need your help."

Twenty-four hours may have been enough for my anger toward Wren to decrease to a simmer, but that was only because I had a new plan.

Operation *Drive Wren So Insane He Quits the Competition* commencing.

"Agent Thomas Angel Jones reporting for duty," I said to the reflection in my bedroom mirror.

I may not have been big and buff like Wren, but I had great assets, with emphasis on the ass, so I picked a pair of white skin-tight jeans I knew would not only show every single curve, but in certain lighting you could see what I had under it. I paired the skinny jeans with a loose crop top that fell off my shoulder.

"Damn, Agent Jones, you're looking fine." If Mason's was my catwalk, I was going to own the fashion show.

Despite my choice of clothing, miles apart from my usual tailored and Coco-approved look, I didn't want to parade around town looking like a Friday night piece of meat looking for some fun.

The chill in the fall air made it more than comfortable to wear a coat that was long enough to cover what I didn't want everyone to see.

"Morning, Indy, can I have the usual coffee and one of those sinful cupcakes, please?"

"Oh hey, hun, sure thing."

He gave me a look as he took my payment card.

"I didn't realize it was that cold outside, maybe we're going to have one of those winters, hey."

"Um, yeah, it's pretty chilly out there."

Just as I said that someone came inside Spilled Beans and took their coat off. "God, I'm so ready for winter. I hate this middle-of-the-road mild."

My cheeks heated, knowing I'd been caught.

"What exactly are you wearing, Tom?"

I opened my coat and gave him my most innocent look. It always worked with Charlie and Gina so I had to try.

"Jesus fucking Christ, Tom, what are you doing dressed like that?" he whispered so his customers didn't hear.

I shrugged and he shook his head.

"Well, whatever you're up to, I want to know later because I bet it's going to be so so good or really bad."

I picked up my coffee and cupcake and gave him an air kiss before I left.

The storeroom was empty when I walked into Mason's through the staff door. Now that I was here I started having doubts. Was this too much? God, I could lose my job.

I looked for a spare shirt that I kept hung behind the office door in case whatever I wore got dirty but then remembered I'd taken it home to wash because I'd already worn it recently. Crap.

Well, if I couldn't do anything about it I may as well own it. It was with that attitude that I walked out into the store and right past Wren, who was checking out a customer's purchase.

My first job of the day was the Pride window. I went over to the window and re-arranged the positioning of the armchair so it would sit in front of the fake fireplace.

"Tom, what are you doing?"

I stopped where I was holding onto the arm of the chair. Wren stood behind me, so I took some time straightening my back and turning around.

Plastering my innocent smile, I said, "I'm dressing the window, can't you see?"

His eyes roamed my body from bottom to top; when they locked on mine I felt as though Wren had his hands on me, for how intense his gaze was.

"I can see."

My cock hardened in my jeans; it was equal measures of pain and pleasure. I wanted to see if I was having the same effect on Wren as he had on me, but I didn't dare move my eyes away from his.

How was he turning the tables on me with one single look when I'd spent hours picking the right outfit just to provoke a reaction?

"Let me know if you need any help with the heavy stuff," he said and turned around toward the back office.

I let out a long breath and sat down on the chair to regain my breath.

What the hell had just happened? And why did he walk away so unaffected when I felt like I'd been run over by a truck?

There was only one explanation. Wren was as straight as an arrow and Indy was totally wrong.

Wren kept out of my way the rest of the day. I'd almost forgotten he was in the store until I was putting the final touches to the window display.

"Wow."

"Holy mother of pearls, warn a girl," I said, clutching the cleaning rag to my chest.

"Sorry," Wren said with a chuckle. "I didn't mean to startle you."

"That's okay. So...what do you think?"

My hands shook as he took everything in. He stepped forward and picked up the framed picture.

Out of everything in the display window I didn't think he'd notice it first.

"This isn't a stock photo."

"Erm, no."

The photo frame was one of Mason's but the photo in it wasn't. I just hoped Wren didn't ask too many questions about it or I'd have to confess to the little personal touch I'd added to the window display.

He looked at me and it was like he saw right into my soul. I'd come in ready for war, and inside I was still mad at Wren for being in the bake-off. Okay, I knew that it was unreasonable to be mad at him, after all, he had the right to enter the competition as much as I did, but with him looking at me like that and the stakes of the competition being so high, at the moment I felt more vulnerable than I had in a long time.

"If it's okay I'm going home a bit early tonight. I have to practice the cupcakes and my back hurts a little from moving all this stuff around."

I started walking toward the storeroom door but stopped when Wren grabbed my hand. He let it go when I turned around, and I missed instantly the too-brief warmth of his skin.

"I get it now," he said in a low voice.

"Get what?"

"Your vision. This"—he held up the photo—"is special, isn't it?"

"Very much."

His smile was like a warm embrace, and I needed to get out of there before I did something weird like hugging him.

"Goodnight, Wren."

"Night, Tom."

When Tom left I went back to the window. I still had the photo in my hand, so I looked closely at it. It was of two men sitting on a sofa next to a fireplace and between them there was a little boy. It was clearly taken at Christmas because even without a Christmas tree, there were plenty of decorations on the mantelpiece above the fireplace.

Tom had confirmed the photo was real. I wondered who was in it. Was this his family? The photo was old so I couldn't see Tom's distinct violet eyes, but I could see the happiness in the child as he looked up at one of the men.

The bell on the door got my attention, and I put the photo back on the mantelpiece of the fake fireplace to go greet my mom, who was walking in with Troy and carrying a bunch of shopping bags.

"We got you everything you need," Mom said.

"Thank you so much, Mom. Did you find all the right colors?"

She gave me a look.

"Of course you did, because you're the best Mom in the world."

"Suck up," Troy coughed and I gave him the finger behind our mom's back.

"Boys!" she chided. "Oh, the window is finished."

She went outside the store and we followed her. We stopped in front of the window but a few steps back. I took it all in the same way customers and visitors would as they walked past.

The scene in front of me was Mason's and it was Pride all in one simple display. I knew now what Tom had tried to capture. There were many LGBTQ families whose lives were no different to anyone else. They watched the same shows on TV, held the same jobs, tried and failed to do the same newspaper crosswords.

There was no need for rainbows or glitter. Sometimes, you are just you.

At the same time this was something many LGBTQ families aspired to have, because they'd been persecuted, discriminated against, couldn't get the jobs or the promotions, found no representation on TV.

I looked at the frame again. It was possibly the smallest item on the display but undoubtedly the most important.

Words I wanted to say became stuck in my throat, and my chest ached with the pain of all the secrets I was keeping.

Was I proud of myself? LGBTQ or not, I lived half a life. It was compartmentalized, and because of this I always felt like it wasn't complete.

"Mom, do you mind closing down for me? I need to do something."

"Of course, honey."

I got in my car and drove off. I tried to call Aiden but the call went straight to voicemail.

The high school parking lot was almost empty so I picked a spot close to the football field and parked. I sat in the car staring outside. So many times in the past I'd done the same but back then I'd been psyching myself up for a game.

Every game had been played as if it was the last one because I'd had no pretense that once high school was over I'd need to focus on college and having a real life.

Except I'd been picked up by a scout and suddenly I'd been looking at a lifetime full of game after game, and I'd never need to worry about not playing again. I'd been living the dream.

My injury had been the stark reminder that every dream could still be shattered. I still remembered every single second of the game that had changed my life twelve years ago when I was only eighteen, but I couldn't even remember who I'd been playing against when I was injured.

I got out of the car toward the football field. The lights were still on, but I didn't see anyone around, so I walked onto the grass toward the center of the field.

The grass smelled fresh like it had just been watered. The field of the Marinos stadium was artificial turf, as were many these days, but I always missed the real grass of my high school field. I hadn't even realized how much until I was standing in it, the smell bringing back all the memories.

"Well if it isn't my best quarterback."

"Coach Johnson. Man, it's been a while."

I gave my old coach a hug and pat on the back.

"Hoping to come back here, son?"

"I'm a little too old, don't you think?" I laughed.

"I mean as a coach."

He said it in such a casual manner, I shook my head and blinked to make sure I understood what he was saying.

"Son, I've been watching you play since you were this high." He put his hand up to his hip. "No way I'd stop just because I'd have to see you on TV."

"So you know about the injury."

He nodded. "When I asked your parents about you they seemed oblivious so I didn't press the matter. I figured you wanted to keep it to yourself until you knew the impact of the injury."

"That was exactly what I did, but then I got the worst news."

"What are you doing now?"

I laughed. "Coaching high school football."

Coach Johnson put his hand on my shoulder and said, "Well, son, if you ever wanted to coach high school, say in a small town, there may be a coach who's reluctant to let go but very much in need of retiring before the Mrs. takes action into her own hands."

"How's Mrs. J.? Does she still make brownies for the team if they win a game?"

"She sure does. I did well when I married that woman. If you haven't found someone like that, you better get on it. Catcha later. Don't want to get late for dinner."

"See ya later, Coach."

"Think about it," he said as he walked off, not bothering to hear my reply.

His words stayed with me well into the night. Not that I'd do anything with them, because as morning came and I had to think about the next stage of the bake-off, I put Coach Johnson's words in a box and placed it somewhere deep inside me to come back to later.

The next challenge of the bake-off was to make rainbow cupcakes. I'd watched countless YouTube videos that explained how to make them, but it didn't make sense to me how it would work. How come the colors didn't mix when they were in the oven? How did they get such neat stripes of color?

I'd played football in front of large crowds since I was a kid, but the prospect of not only baking but decorating the cupcakes live and in front of an audience made me break out into a sweat.

I followed my mom's recipe for the vanilla sponge we'd made the other day. The batter looked the same as before. So far, so good. Then came the hard part.

Separating the batter into six equal portions was a mathematical challenge because I didn't have enough bowls, so I had to be creative, but it meant figuring out how much was in each container when all the containers measured differently.

Once the batter was done I lined up the cupcake paper cases in the tin. My mom had given me hers, saying that way the cupcakes wouldn't spread out.

Opening the little tubes of food coloring should have been its own challenge in the competition because no matter how much I tried, the plastic tips just wouldn't bend and snap as it said on the picture.

"Right, teeth it is, and if I need a trip to the dentist after this I better win the damned competition."

I bit the tip of the tube and bent it until I heard it snap, and a bit of liquid dripped from my mouth. Fuck, I hoped to god I hadn't broken a tooth. I ran my hand over my mouth and it came back red.

My first instinct was to run to the bathroom to check my lip, but I wasn't in any pain, which was when I realized that I'd opened the tube with the red food coloring and now had spread it over my face with my hands.

I squirted a few drops inside one of the containers and stirred until the batter turned into a pink-ish shade. Unsure if it was safe to add more color, I left it as it was.

One by one I managed to open all the tubes, with various results. I had six containers of rainbow colors, and I also had food coloring all over my face, arms, and I was pretty sure there was some in my hair too.

Six layers of batter later and the cupcakes were ready to go in the oven.

Time to clear up the mess and look in the mirror to assess the damage.

There was a knock on the door as I was on my way to the bathroom, but since it could only be someone in my family I didn't think twice about opening it.

I was already preparing myself to be the butt of family jokes for years to come when I opened the door and came face-to-face with Tom.

"Oh my god, what happened, are you hurt?"

He touched my face, his fingers rubbing my lip. There was nothing but concern in his eyes, but my traitorous dick decided something else was going on.

"No, it's just food coloring."

Tom stood back and I knew he was only now seeing the various patches of color all over me.

He put a hand over his mouth and closed his eyes. His shoulders shook.

"Wait, are you laughing at me?"

"No." He coughed. "Of course...not."

Even as he said it he started laughing aloud. I pulled him inside and closed the door.

"Is there anything I can help you with? Or do you just need me for your own entertainment?" I tried to sound incensed, but I would have added additional patches of food coloring if I could keep seeing Tom laughing like this.

His face lit up, and his eyes were bright with tears. He looked so fucking beautiful.

"I'm sorry, it's not funny, and I shouldn't laugh."

"Nah, it is funny. You should have seen when I nearly cracked a tooth opening the damned tubes."

"Smells nice here, have you got a batch in the oven?"

"Yeah. I'm really nervous about doing it in front of people," I said, running my hands through my hair and coming out with colored streaks on my palms. I sighed.

"As Coco said, *you only live once; you might as well be amusing.* Make that happen," he said, gesturing to my colored patches, "and they'll love you."

"Maybe you're right."

Tom smiled and I couldn't stop smiling back. I became very aware of his presence so close to me. Blood flowed faster through my veins and made me feel dizzy; my breath caught and my fingers itched to touch him.

I raised my hand to his cheek but stopped before I could actually touch him. His mouth opened slightly and his eyes closed. His chest raised and deflated as if he was consciously making sure air flowed through his lungs or he'd faint.

The sound of a car starting outside startled us and in the moment I took my hand back.

"I—" My words were stuck in my throat. Not that I had a chance to say anything before Tom spoke.

"Here," he said, stretching out his hand to give me an envelope. "Abi asked me to stop by to give you this on the way home." And then he left.

My parents' place was in no way on the route to Tom's place. Why had he come here?

The buzzer went off so I closed the door and picked up a dish towel to check on the cupcakes. They were clearly over baked. How was I ever going to win that competition? And was it even the competition I wanted to win anymore?

Fuck.

TOM

I couldn't believe I'd nearly kissed Wren.

His reaction to my window had been on replay on my mind, like a circular catwalk but where there was no change in clothing. Then Abi wouldn't stop telling me all these cute stories about him that didn't match at all the persona he seemed to put up around me.

When she'd asked me to deliver an envelope with documents to Wren I couldn't say no, after all she was my boss. But she'd dressed it like it was only a small detour on my way home when it was nothing but. I hadn't realized until I was nearly there that the address she'd given me was their address but for a separate apartment above the garage.

I'd decided to just put the letter in the mailbox but then there wasn't one, and I didn't know how important the documents were. As a last attempt I'd rung the bell on the main house, hoping Troy would be in but there had been no answer.

Abi had told me that Jonas had started going for small walks around the block with Troy to build up his strength, so

I'd been left with no choice but to knock on the door of the apartment.

After witnessing Jonas's heart attack, when I saw Wren covered in red I'd panicked and then couldn't stop laughing when he'd clarified it was food coloring.

I'd had my own struggles with the food coloring tubes sold in the grocery store, but Indy had said to use scissors to cut through the plastic lid to make it easier to snap. My food coloring disaster had been contained to the kitchen work surface.

As soon as I'd recovered from the laughing fit, I'd become very aware of how close we'd been to each other and how Wren's gaze burned into my skin.

I didn't know what had been going through his head but inside mine there had been a giant flashing billboard saying *kiss him, kiss him.* As he'd raised his hand to nearly cup my face, I'd known I was going to do it, but fortunately a car noise outside had brought me to my senses.

I shouldn't kiss him because he was straight—even if I had my doubts about that at the moment—but at least he was in the closet and there was no way I'd be with someone who wasn't out. Then there was the fact he was my boss and that there was a whole country between us.

And then there was that itty bitty detail of him being my rival at the bake-off. I hadn't paid any attention to the other contestants that first day of the bake-off, something I now regretted because I had no clue who my competition was.

When I walked back into the high school gym I was a ball of nerves. I was afraid that all the crap going through my head would screw up my concentration, and I was even more afraid that my competition was just too good. I had so much riding on this bake-off, I didn't even want to consider how I'd feel if I didn't win.

There were three rows of worktops, and as I approached I saw there were name cards at each end, so I looked for mine.

A girl with long blonde hair tied in two braids on either side of her head smiled at me.

"Hi, I'm Amy, is this nerve-racking or what?" She held the end of one of her braids and started playing with it.

"Oh god, yeah, I couldn't even sleep last night," I said. "I'm Tom."

I found my name and started looking at the items on the top. We could practice the challenges in our own time but for the bake-off days they provided us with all the ingredients. A quick assessment reassured me I had everything I'd asked for.

The other contestants came in shortly after, as well as the supporters who had started filling the bleachers on either side. I was glad the organizers got our stations to face the door rather than the bleachers, because it was easier to ignore the crowd if it was in my periphery.

I heard my name being called and looked to see who it was. Halfway up the bleachers, sitting all in a row, I saw Indy, Ellie, Ben, Tristan, and Connor. I ran up to greet them.

"If you're coming to witness my humiliation you better have fully charged batteries on your cellphones," I joked, but they all took their phones out of their pockets and looked at them.

"Traitors."

"Not at all," Ellie said. "Charlie made us promise we'd send him some videos."

"Yes, he did." Connor nodded.

I shook my head in mock indignation, but in reality I'd never felt so part of something, and it made my chest swell. I needed to go back to my station before I started hugging everybody and ugly crying.

Ugly crying didn't go with my rainbow vest. Fact.

As I walked back to my station I saw Wren standing next to it.

"Hey," he said. He smiled but it didn't reach his eyes, and his fingers were doing a great job of wringing themselves into a knot.

"Hey."

"Erm, my family wanted to come to support us," he said.

I looked at the bleachers in the direction Wren looked, and there, right on the front row, was Troy, Abi, and Jonas.

Troy waved and I ran over to greet them.

"Can't believe you're making me come to school on a non-school day," Troy said, looking irritated.

"Shut up, I know you come to school after hours all the time. And there's no cake in the computer lab." I winked.

"What, we can eat your cupcakes when you're finished?"

"Yup."

"See, Mom? This is why I said we should come."

Both Abi and Jonas laughed. I gave Abi a quick hug and moved on to Jonas.

"Hey, Jonas, how are you doing?"

"I'm good, son, thank you for keeping things ticking along for me."

I gave him another hug and went back to my station with a frog in my throat. If only Jonas knew how much it meant to me every time he called me son, even if he himself didn't mean anything by it.

Wren looked a little calmer when I got back to the station, but I didn't understand why he was still there. My confusion must have been clear because he said, "We're sharing stations."

"Oh, okay."

By the time the challenge started the gym was full of spectators. I tried not to look at anyone. This wasn't just about the rainbow color of the cupcake. I needed the flavor and texture to be good too.

I willed my nerves away by replaying an interview I'd watched with Coco Chanel a few weeks ago in my head.

Everything went silent around me but the voice of Coco talking about her new collection. Next thing I knew, my batter was done, colored, and the cupcakes went in the oven.

The woman presenting the challenge made some comments about what she was observing, and the crowd was mostly silent. I looked around and saw my friends giving me a thumbs up. I smiled and waved at them.

Next to me there was a crash, and it was the first time since I'd found out I was sharing the work space with Wren that I'd been aware of him there.

His cheeks were flushed and he looked stressed. There was color inside the bowls, outside the bowls, and on his apron. Thankfully not on his face this time.

I saw his hands shake as he spooned each color in turn inside the cupcake case, and then he put his tray in the oven.

Once he was done, he put his hands on the worktop and stretched his back, taking a deep sigh. He looked at me with a strained smile and then we both looked at the other contestants.

Everyone seemed to have their cupcakes in the oven too and were clearing up.

There was a break in the competition once we took the cupcakes out to let them cool before they were decorated. The organizers had set up one of the locker rooms as a rest area for us.

I took a bottle of water but ignored the various snacks on the table in the corner. Amy filled a plate and then sat next to me.

"So glad they have food. I was so nervous I skipped dinner last night and didn't have breakfast either."

An older man sat on a bench opposite us.

"Why can't we talk during the challenge? My wife helped me practice all the steps out loud. I'm sure I forgot something, but hey, I have six cupcake-looking stripy things in there."

I raised my water and Amy her plate. In the anticipation of the challenge I'd forgotten we were all very much amateurs.

"I'm Phil by the way," he said.

"Hi, Phil, I'm Tom and this is Amy."

I didn't see the other two contestants, a really young girl and an older woman. Wren sat away from us on his cellphone. As if he knew my eyes were on him, he looked up and frowned when his eyes met mine. I looked away and continued chatting to Amy and Phil.

The decoration part of the challenge was fun. I'd seen this video on the internet on how to make a rainbow effect on buttercream and had practiced a little at home. It hadn't always worked so I prayed it did now that it really counted.

I sneaked a peak at Wren's side of the station, and he looked more focused than earlier, but it looked like he was mixing the colors of the buttercream to make new colors. Had he run out of food coloring?

We weren't allowed to talk to each other so I did a little cough and he looked at me. I used my eyes to point at my tubes, and he gave me the tiniest smile and picked up the tubes that were right in the middle of the station. I hoped no one had noticed our communication.

Once again the judging was done blind, so we went back to the locker room while the judges worked out their scores. This time Wren sat next to me but he kept to himself. I took that as his own way of thanking me for the buttercream save.

His piping work was different from mine but the colors

were right and I thought his cupcakes looked pretty and delicious. Amy's looked stunning. She'd added glitter spray so her cupcakes were all shiny. Why hadn't I thought of that?

Never mind, I was still happy with how my attempt at rainbow swirls had come out.

When we were called back for the results the gym hall was buzzing with excitement. There were cheers for all the contestants, and I didn't miss the mayor's relief that no incidents had happened.

"Ladies and gentleman. It has been indeed a colorful challenge, but we can all agree our contestants couldn't have done it better. In fact, they should be very *proud* of themselves." the presenter said, letting out a belly laugh at his own joke. "So without further ado let's get the results."

The crowd stamped their feet on the bleachers like a drum roll.

"In first place, and with a guaranteed place in the next round, we have...Tom Jones."

Had he said my name? Like for real? He must have because the cheers from Ben, Travis, Connor, and Ellie were loud enough I'd hear them from my apartment. I saw that Hannah had joined them and was waving with one hand while she had her cellphone pointed toward me, clearly filming the results.

Amy came second and then Phil, and then the younger girl who was called Bea. My heart beat hard in my chest. I didn't think Wren's cupcakes looked all that bad. Even though we were technically rivals, there was part of me that didn't want him to leave the competition just yet.

"And the last person to join us for the next round is...Wren Mason."

There were cheers all round, no doubt from loyal Mason's customers. He went back to his family, who were standing and cheering, and I went up the bleachers to celebrate with my cheerleaders.

I hadn't reached the second row when someone pulled me by my arm. It was the older lady, Gladys, who'd missed out on a place.

"I'd like to congratulate you and also warn you."

"Thanks, and excuse me?"

She looked over at Wren, who spotted me from the other side of the hall and waved.

"I'd be careful of him if I were you. He made some comments earlier and I wouldn't be surprised if he accused you of cheating."

I wanted to ask her what she meant, but a guy around my age interrupted us to take her home.

WREN

Who would have known I'd spent most of my life competing against others? No one, because in that gym hall, with all those people watching, I'd lost it completely. Thank god for best friends and pep talks.

Aiden had calmed me down and reminded me I was used to finding focus while surrounded by people. He was right, and that's what I'd done for the second half of the challenge.

Unfortunately, somehow between the first and second half, a couple of my food coloring tubes had gone missing. I figured I'd mix the colors to make the ones I didn't have, which would have worked out if I was trying to create anything that wasn't a rainbow.

I could have kissed Tom right there and then for helping me, but we weren't allowed to talk. I'd gone through to the next round but it had been too close a call.

After the results I'd wanted to thank Tom, but my dad had been getting tired so we'd gone home. I figured I could see Tom at the store the next day.

I was in the shower when there was a persistent knock on the door. Worried that there may be something wrong with my dad, I got out of the shower and put a towel around my waist to go answer the door.

As soon as I unlocked it the door pushed open and a whirlwind of Tom barreled in, stopping by the sofa that divided the kitchen and living area of the small space.

"What kind of game are you playing?" Tom asked.

"I don't know what you're talking about."

"I haven't cheated, and I would never cheat, do you hear me?" He came at me, pointing his finger. He looked furious and for the life of me I had no clue what I'd done.

"Do you think they'll accuse us of cheating because I used your food coloring?"

"What? No, they didn't notice that."

"Then I don't know what you're talking about."

He crossed his arms and pursed his lips and then huffed and put his hands on his hips.

Suddenly, I was very aware that I was stood right in front of a man I was ridiculously attracted to and I was only wearing a towel. He didn't seem to notice because he carried on.

"Gladys warned me about you. Are you going to deny that you have plans to get me kicked out?"

"You're going to have to tell me a bit more about what's behind this, and what the hell did Gladys tell you?"

"Ha! Wouldn't you want to know."

"Yes, actually. If I'm being accused of something I didn't do, I deserve a chance to defend myself."

He seemed to think about it. His hands went back on his hips, and I bit the inside of my cheek so I wouldn't smile. No doubt that wouldn't have gone down well. And why the fuck was I getting aroused by his little display?

"Gladys said you made some comments earlier about me, and she said I should be careful that you might accuse me of cheating."

It all made sense then. I took a deep breath and considered how to explain it in a way Tom would believe me. "She spoke to me earlier. Her grandson, Zack, was in the football team at school, but he was a year older than me. When he got kicked out of the team I got his place. I didn't know at the time why he was kicked out, but his family had hopes he'd make it pro and blamed me for taking his spot."

"How would that be your fault?"

"Coach Johnson was always very strict with us. If we wanted to be on the team we needed to get the grades too. I think Zack was struggling, and apparently he cheated on a test to get the grades. Zack thought I was the one to tell Coach J. but I wasn't."

Tom narrowed his eyes as if he was trying to absorb the information I'd just given him.

"I'm sorry, Tom. Maybe Gladys was upset that she didn't make it, but I swear, I would never cheat in a competition, and I would definitely never do anything to put your place in jeopardy."

He ran his hands through his hair, something I'd never seen him do before, and sat on the sofa. I sat next to him and reached out to touch his leg.

"Are we okay?"

He looked at me and suddenly his eyes went wide open.

"You're naked. How long have you been naked?"

I chuckled. "All the time you've stood here?"

His eyes roamed my body, and I swore I felt them on my skin as he kept looking down. My nipples hardened and my stomach tightened. I knew my secret was going to be out in moments, but I didn't care anymore. In fact, I anticipated it with excitement.

Tom's breath became shallower as his eyes reached my waist. The towel had opened slightly but I was still covered up.

Not for long though, because my cock was hardening at lightning speed and it wouldn't be contained if he kept looking at me like that.

"Tom." My voice was croaky and lust-filled. His pupils were so dilated his eyes looked nearly black. He wanted me as much as I wanted him, and there was only one way to jump through the hurdle of my secret.

Without thinking too much about it, I put one hand on the back of his neck and the other on his cheek and pressed my lips to his.

Tom let out a little sigh, but the kiss didn't last more than a few seconds before he pulled back. His chest was heaving and his mouth parted like he was trying to take a much-needed breath. "What was that?"

"That was me kissing you, Tom."

"Why did you kiss me?"

"Because I wanted to."

"Why?"

"Do you want me to number the reasons?" I asked, raising my hands to count them out. "Number one: you're sexy as fuck. Number two: I can't resist when you're all angry. Number three: you looked like you wanted it too. Number four: have I mentioned how much *I wanted to*? Number five—"

I was interrupted by Tom throwing himself at me with such force I ended up lying on the couch with him on top of me. The kiss was a mix of angry and desperate, his hands were everywhere they could reach on my body, and I couldn't stop the sound that came out when I opened my mouth and Tom plunged in.

Tom tasted sweet, like he'd had one of the cupcakes we'd made earlier, and my head filled with thoughts of licking that fucking rainbow buttercream off his body.

There was no hope in hell of keeping my towel closed. With every move of his hips my cock rubbed against the fabric of his pants. Tom was as hard as I was, and I was pretty sure he could feel me too.

God, his lips were addictive, but I wanted more. I licked and kissed his cheek, moving slowly toward his neck where I couldn't resist sucking the skin just behind his ear. He let out a little moan.

"Hmm so good, I want to taste you everywhere," I said, licking his Adam's apple and paying attention to the other side of his neck.

"This... this isn't happening, right?"

I chuckled. "Why do you say that?"

He put his hands on my chest to prop himself up a little. "You're not gay."

"I'm bi."

"But everybody thinks you're straight. I mean, people don't really talk about your sexuality behind your back, but I've never heard anyone mention you dating guys."

"That's because I rarely dated before I went to college, and because I liked girls too, I guess I never felt the need to come out."

"Oh."

He sat up, leaving me completely exposed, in more ways than one. I grabbed the towel and covered myself up again.

"I am going to come out to my family, but I guess I got too wrapped up with my life in San Diego and never got to it. Now the priority is making sure my dad is okay and keeping the store going." I put a hand on his cheek, rubbing his soft skin. "But, Tom, I am going to come out, and I'm not saying it to make any kind of promises. I think it's clear we're both attracted to each other, so I just want you to know that *I am* into guys, you're not the first, and I will tell my family when I'm ready."

There was reluctance in his eyes but I could see he wanted this as much as I did.

"You don't have to come out because of me." He said the words but there was no conviction behind them.

"You're right, I will come out because I want to do it, for me, for my family, and for the future I want to have."

He nodded. "So all the times you looked like you couldn't stand me—"

I put my finger on his lips. "It was because I wanted you." And then replaced them with my mouth again.

Tom's smaller frame against mine was a perfect fit, as though we'd been made to spend the rest of our lives like this.

I chased the errant thought from my head to focus on the here and now.

"So you're okay with me kissing you?"

He nodded and smiled a truly genuine Tom smile.

"There's very little I'd be more okay with," he said, sucking the skin on my neck, which would probably leave a mark. My cock throbbed at the thought.

TOM

When I'd gone to Wren's place the plan had been to get him to confess and find out if what Gladys had said was true. I couldn't have predicted a more different kind of confession.

Kissing Wren had been unexpected. Hell, I hadn't seen it coming, especially as I hadn't been the one to initiate it. If anything, I'd thought if it ever happened it would be because I'd finally let go of my self-restraint and gone for it, knowing the straight man would at best reject me gently.

Wren was bisexual. It made sense now, the way he'd said *we* when he'd mentioned people come in all colors, shapes, and sizes when referring to LGBTQ people.

The funny thing was, I think I already knew it, but hadn't wanted to trust my gut feeling in case it was wrong.

After our conversation I'd ended up once again on top of Wren, getting acquainted with his lips. We'd talked some more, while I'd explored every inch of his hard chest. The man had grooves and ridges that went on for days, and had I wanted to take things further there was nothing I'd love to do more than lick every single one of them.

We'd both been very hard and I'd known it wouldn't have taken much for both of us to come with a few expert strokes or licks, but it was too early. We'd just discovered...us, and I didn't want the post-climax head to ruin the moment.

After Wren had finally put some clothes on we'd watched a movie together and then I'd come home, where I'd gone straight to the shower to take care of my earlier problem, one that was still persistent when morning came. Pun intended.

"Damn you, I have to go to work. Just because he's not the ice man anymore it doesn't give you permission to get all perky."

In the battle of wills my cock won and nearly made me late for work, so I didn't have time to stop at Spilled Beans for my usual morning coffee.

I knew not having a coffee before work was a bad decision. I should have just apologized to Wren for my lateness and got us both a coffee, because neither of us had a moment to breathe all morning.

I'd come back to the storeroom to look for a Tupperware box for Mrs. Jenkins for the third time when I was pushed up against the shelf and felt a set of lips on my neck.

"Fuck, I've been wanting to do this all morning," Wren said, untucking my shirt and his hands roaming over my chest.

"Don't we have a store full of people out there?" I asked, not really caring what the answer was as I turned around to kiss him properly.

"We do, but at the moment I could kiss Mrs. Jenkins for being so picky with her boxes."

"No kissing Mrs. Jenkins. Her breath smells of cat hair."

"Ew."

"Wren..."

"Hmm."

His bigger heavy body pressing me against the shelves was doing all kinds of things to me, so before I pulled my pants down and begged him to fuck me right there, I put a hand between our mouths.

I felt him smile and then lick my palm, which of course might as well have been directly on my dick.

"Mr. Mason, we have customers outside."

He took a deep breath and straightened up his clothes. I tucked my shirt back in and picked a number of boxes for Mrs. Jenkins to justify the length of time I'd been gone.

"Oh no, dear, these won't do either. They're not the right size," Mrs. Jenkins said for the dozenth time.

"What is it exactly you want the box for? Maybe if I have an idea I can look for options at the back?"

She looked around and then came closer and whispered, "It's for my late husband's ashes."

I didn't want to state the obvious that any shape and size would do, so I thought of a different question.

"Okay, so what is your ideal size and shape?"

"My David always said that if he ended up in a box it would need to be long enough for...you know..."

I stared at her before I understood what she meant.

"Oh...oh! And um...how big was...he?"

"Nine inches when he was...well, excited. But he was quite girthy."

I coughed to stop from laughing.

"And you want a box that can accommodate David while erm, excited or..."

"Maybe best, dear, we wouldn't want things to get uncomfortable in there."

"Okay, do you want to take a seat over there by the window and I'll go see what I can find for you?"

She patted my hand. "Oh you're a good boy."

I couldn't stop my laugh as soon as the door closed and I was safely out of earshot.

Wren came out from the office holding a small delivery box.

"What's so funny?"

"You don't want to know."

He raised a brow.

"Fine, you asked for it. I've spent the last thirty minutes looking for a box that can accommodate the length and girth of Mr. Jenkins's erect penis. But apparently while he may be picky about the size of the box, he doesn't mind that it's plastic with a tight seal lock."

"Didn't Mr. Jenkins die like ten years ago?"

"Yes, but apparently the seal on the old box is damaged, and she's afraid of moisture getting in."

He shook his head and made a move to leave but not without pressing me against the door and kissing me again.

Being busy at least made the day go fast because in between stolen kisses and demanding customers I almost didn't notice it was closing time.

I flipped the sign on the door and locked it while Wren cashed up, and then did a once through around the store to face up the stock. I'd had no coffee all day and still felt perky and happy. *Wren Mason, what are you doing to me?*

"Hopefully you, if you want to come home with me," he said, putting his arms around me and kissing my nose.

"Did I say that out loud?"

"Uh huh."

"Then I guess you have your answer."

"Let's go."

～

Okay, when a guy asks you to come home with him and he's been stealing kisses all day and groping your ass every chance he gets, you might assume what's in store for you.

Practicing doughnuts for the next challenge wasn't quite what I had in mind, even if it was the most sensible thing to do.

"Stop looking like a kicked puppy," Wren said, reaching out for my hand and placing a kiss on the palm. "You have no idea how much self-restraint I need to not jump you right now, but we need to practice this."

"Fine."

"Okay, the ingredients are all measured. Do you want to read out the recipe and I'll do it?"

"Sure."

I picked up the piece of paper with the recipe and sat on a stool on the other side of the counter and read out the instructions. For the other challenges the organizers had allowed us to pick our own recipe, but they had insisted that for this one we needed to all follow the same one.

"It doesn't seem too complicated, does it?" I asked.

"No, I think the challenge will be in the kneading of the dough and then not burning them in the fryer."

When the dough was well mixed Wren put some flour on the worktop and we each took turns kneading the dough so I had a chance to feel the texture.

"So now the recipe says it needs to rest for one hour."

Wren put the dough in the bowl and covered it with plastic wrap. Then he looked at me.

"What?" I checked the recipe to make sure I hadn't skipped any steps.

"Now is the part that we won't be doing on the live show." He came around the counter and placed himself between my legs. I yelped when he picked me up without warning and only had time to hold on to his broad shoulders and tighten my legs around his waist before we were on the move.

I sucked on his pulse point and felt his throat vibrating from his groan as I licked and nibbled my way round his neck.

He stopped and pushed me against the wall. "Keep your legs tight around me." Then he laced his hands with mine and pinned them above my head on the wall and pressed his lips against mine.

"I didn't see any marks on you today," he said.

I'd only ever seen Wren clean-shaven, but he probably hadn't shaved today because the short scruff rubbing against my skin was lighting all my senses.

"I...erm...makeup," I tried to articulate. God, this man had the power to render me speechless, which was a true skill, and I wasn't even naked.

He kissed me again and pulled back, his blue eyes inviting me to get lost in them.

"Cheeky. After what you've just done I think I might need some myself tomorrow."

I bit my lip and batted my eyelids.

"Sorry?"

He laughed but then he looked to the door to the left of us. I saw a bed and a chest of drawers next to it. I released one of my hands from his light hold and cradled his face. He looked at me with uncertainty.

"I would love to," I whispered into his lips.

"What exactly?"

"Anything, Wren. With you, anything."

We kissed our way into the bedroom, not bothering to close the door. Well, I didn't do anything but allow myself to be carried and then placed on the bed.

Wren's bigger, heavier body pinned me in place as his mouth claimed mine and his hands got busy undressing me.

"I've waited all day to have you like this," he said between open-mouthed kisses on my neck and chest.

"Oh yeah? And what are you going to do with me?"

"I'm going to drive you so crazy you won't even remember your favorite color."

I laughed. "Too late, and it's black. You're going to have to up your game with me Mr." I lifted my hips to help him get rid of my slacks.

Wren licked a path from my toe all the way to my underwear. My cock was stupidly hard and I nearly came when he licked and then sucked the little wet spot over my crown.

"Holy glitterballs." I panted.

"I hope not, that shit gets everywhere." He chuckled.

My skin was on fire under Wren's expert touch. I didn't even know where to put my hands: over my mouth to silence my moans or on his head to encourage him to pull my underwear down and take my desperate cock in his mouth.

"Fuck, Wren, I need more."

"More what, baby?"

"More you, on me. Skin," I growled. "I need you fucking inside me."

He covered my body with his again.

"This is it, baby. This is how I want you. So desperate for me." And then he claimed my mouth as he wrapped his hands around my cock.

"I've been desperate for you since I smelled your cologne that first day. Even when I didn't know anything about you I felt like my body wanted you already."

Wren reached out for the side table and grabbed a condom and a small bottle of lube.

"Fucking finally. I thought I was going to need to summon the unicorn gods."

His stare had enough heat to pin me in place, even if I just couldn't resist reaching out for my cock while Wren suited up and added some lube to the condom and then his fingers.

"Confession time," I said, trying to don my sprinkles-wouldn't-melt face.

Wren raised a brow but he found out my secret as soon as one of his fingers entered my tight heat.

"You're prepped." He raised my legs to have a closer look at my pre-lubed hole and then looked at me, his finger going back to the job it had been doing seconds ago.

I bit my lip and closed my eyes, trying to stifle a moan as his fingers found my prostate.

"Jesus fuck, just put it in me. Please."

The short-lived pain of adjusting to Wren's size was so welcome I could have cried for him to push harder. I knew I wouldn't last long.

Despite the times I'd made myself come in the shower to images of Wren in my mind, the real thing was a million rainbow years better.

"Tom," Wren moaned against the crook of my neck where he sucked on my skin.

I felt the tension in the muscles of his back as my hands tried to cover as much of him as they could.

"Please, Wren, I need to come," I begged.

"Yes...hmm...fuck, yes."

He put his hands under my back and raised my hips to meet each of his thrusts. The position caused his cock to pass over my prostate with every single movement.

I'd never passed out from an orgasm before, but there was a first for everything.

When I came to I was clean, warm, and settled against

Wren's hard chest. I knew he was awake from the gentle way he was running his fingers through my hair.

We stayed like that for a few minutes. This was normally the time I'd fall asleep but this moment was too precious to lose to unconsciousness.

"Tom, can I ask you a question?"

My head rested on Wren's chest and I played with his blond hairs, feeling as his chest rose up and down with each breath, or caught when I was too close to his nipple.

"Uh huh," was all I was capable of since the movements of his chest were rapidly sending me to sleep in my post-orgasmic bliss.

"Why did you enter the bake-off?"

"I need the prize money," I said with a yawn. Wren moved so we were face-to-face.

"Are you in trouble or something?" The concern in his eyes made my heart swell, among other parts of my body.

I smiled. "No. Nothing like that. I'm just chasing my dream."

Wren ran his fingers through my hair gingerly. "And what dream is that, baby?"

"I want to rent that empty unit next to Bookmarked and open my own fashion store. All I ever wanted was to work dressing people, make them feel good about themselves so they can go out there and conquer the world." I looked away when I realized I'd said too much.

Wren tilted my head back up so our eyes met again.

"It's a beautiful dream, Tom, and I can really see you do something like that. You were amazing with that guy in the store."

"I thought you were mad because I didn't sell him anything."

He kissed me gently and something inside me changed.

"No, baby. I just couldn't react to it the way I wanted to."

"How...how did you want to react?"

"Like this."

With every pass of Wren's tongue over mine the little glitter snow globe inside my belly shook. I liked that feeling.

WREN

It took me a few seconds when I woke to figure out why I wasn't in my favorite alone sleeping position, and that was because I wasn't alone.

Snoring lightly and snuggled with his back against my chest was Tom. He was using one of my arms as a pillow and the other was snuggled between his arms. We couldn't have been closer without me actually being inside him.

If my morning wood had been at half-mast, then my last thought had done the trick to get it all the way up, and as it was nested between Tom's ass and his lower back, I wouldn't have to do much to get some much-needed friction.

I wanted to touch him, play with his hair, and admire him while he slept, but our position made it impossible. Both my hands were trapped and he was facing the wall, but there was a part of him I could reach that I'd found out last night drove him crazy.

Tom's snores stopped and his breathing pattern changed as I kissed the back of his neck. I felt the small hairs rise under my lips and his body trembled slightly. The giveaway that he was finally awake was that he pushed his ass back.

"Are you going to finish what you started last night?" he asked. His voice still raspy from sleep.

"I thought we finished last night. And quite satisfactorily, if I remember well." My dick twitched against his back.

He turned around and hooked his leg over my hip. His cock was as hard as mine and I remembered how it had felt in my mouth last night when he'd come to the most colorful array of slurs I'd ever heard in my life.

"You look so gorgeous when you come," I said, taking his lips between mine and biting lightly before kissing it better.

"You know what to do if you want a repeat show," he said, pushing his hips so his cock was trapped between us. Then he took his hand from where it was resting on my hip and opened his ass cheeks so my cock naturally drifted between the space.

"Fuck." I groaned.

"Yes, that's right."

We teased each other until we were both breathless and needing more.

I looked at the clock on the side table and I knew we wouldn't have enough time.

"Come have a shower with me," I said.

"Noooo, I want more of this, you." He moaned.

"I'll make it worth your while." I grabbed my cock and rubbed it against his hole, feeling him relax around the head as if he could take it in.

He got up with reluctance, but when he saw the size of my shower, and that it had a bench, he grinned and turned the water on.

Once the water was warm enough we stepped in. Tom looked even more adorable all wet, and I took much pleasure in kissing as much of his skin as I could.

He reached over for the soap. "Sorry, this isn't the one you like, but you'll have to agree with me this situation is much preferable."

"Tom, are you talking to your cock?" I laughed.

"Yes, don't you talk to yours?"

"Only when I'm on my own."

"Well, mine isn't shy, as you can tell."

We both looked down and I hummed my appreciation. Tom had a gorgeous cock, long and thin, framed by a small thatch of trimmed hair. I took the soap from his hand and lathered it between mine before reaching out to his cock.

"Hmm, fuck yes. God, your hands have the same magic powers as your mouth."

"You haven't seen anything yet, baby."

I turned him around to face the tiled wall. The water cascaded down his body like a piece of art, and if I wasn't so desperate to see him come I'd have stood back just watching him until the water ran cold.

I lathered more soap in my hands and massaged his back slowly. Every time he pushed to meet my hands I pushed him right back against the wall.

"Wren, I should tell you this is doing it for me...very much."

"Good to know." I let my cock rub up and down his crease, passing over his hole. He trembled under my touch, pushing back, wanting more.

I never stopped massaging his back until I reached a point I couldn't do it standing up.

"Keep your hands on the wall and don't touch yourself," I said in his ear, finishing with a bite and pull of his earlobe.

I went down on my knees and massaged the globes of his ass. He opened his legs wider and I could see his cock hard and throbbing.

Tom had the cutest perky ass I'd ever seen, but it was when I pushed his cheeks apart and saw my prize that I knew I'd hit the jackpot.

I sucked on his balls and then licked all the way up to his hole, kissing it and sucking as if I was making love to his mouth.

"Holy sacred unicorns, do that again," he pleaded.

So I did, repeatedly, until Tom came apart in my mouth without touching himself.

As soon as he came I stood up and held him close to me. He tried to turn around, but I kept him in place. I stroked my cock over his crease and came seconds later.

The water washed away all the evidence but there was no denying what had happened from our flushed skins and strained breath. A ding from my cellphone in the bedroom reminded me of the outside world, so we finished the shower quickly, stealing a few kisses along the way.

"Oh crap, we totally forgot about the doughnuts last night," Tom said while getting dressed.

I looked up from his ass to his frowning face and shrugged.

"You have a nice ass, sue me." Tom stared at me but I could tell he wasn't against what we'd ended up doing last night. "Okay, okay, how about we practice the doughnuts tonight at yours?"

"Yeah, let's do that. No distractions," Tom said, placing his hands on his hips and attempting a serious face.

I walked over to him and kissed the frown off his face, reassuring him we would have time to practice. Luckily, because of other school events, we had a bigger break between the last challenge and the next one.

"Come on, I'll buy you a coffee at Spilled Beans on the way to the store," I said.

I checked my cellphone for the text message that came earlier and nearly dropped it on the floor.

Dear Mr. Mason. Due to unforeseen circumstances we had to change the date of the next challenge. It will now take place this afternoon. We apologize for the inconvenience. The Pride bake-off organizers.

"What's up?" Tom asked.

"Check your phone in case mine is a glitch."

Tom walked over to the counter where he'd left his phone last night.

"Fuck! How is this possible?"

"I don't know, but I guess they didn't see it coming either."

"But we're working, and we didn't practice the doughnuts all the way to the end."

Tom walked back and forth in the small space between the counter and the sofa, wringing his hands together.

"Hey, hey," I said, stepping in front of him and cradling his face in my hands. "We'll be okay. Trust me?"

He nodded.

I went over to my parents' and found my mom having her breakfast in the kitchen.

"Mom, I need your help. We just got a text from the organizers to say they're moving the next round to this afternoon because someone double booked the gym hall."

"Don't worry, I'll cover in the store. It'll be good for your dad to do his walk in the morning anyway."

"Thanks, Mom." I gave her a kiss on the cheek and left.

Tom sat on the sofa, his hands on his knees like he was ready to fight or flight.

"Mom is covering us in the store this afternoon. It's going to be fine, okay?"

When he looked at me his beautiful violet eyes were shiny.

"This is too important to me, Wren."

"I know, baby. You're good with instructions. We'll go over the recipe again and look up some videos on the internet when we get to the store. You'll be fine."

He nodded and I pulled him in for a strong hug. I knew we were competing against each other but in that moment he looked so upset I would have done anything to see him smile again.

The last-minute change in the date of the next round of the bake-off meant there weren't as many people in the gym watching us. That was the only benefit of the change because as soon as we got to our stations and I looked at the recipe my heart dropped.

Tom must have thought the same; I could read it in his tense frame. They'd changed the recipe on us. Because we had less time in the hall, they wanted us to use one that didn't require proofing.

All the videos we'd watched in the store all morning suddenly became useless. We stared at each other until he looked away to go back to the recipe.

The rest of the afternoon was a blur. I tried my best to follow the recipe but when it came to using the deep fryer I panicked. All the stories about things going wrong for previous contestants ran through my head. Fire. Accidents. Emergency rooms.

If I didn't fry the doughnuts I would definitely lose the round. I thought about my dad's slow recovery from his heart operation, and my mom managing the store all on her own. What if the checkout computer broke down? They literally had no room to move and were relying on the steady income of the store.

And now they were relying on me to do my best to win the prize.

It was with shaking hands that I slowly lowered my first doughnut into the deep fryer.

TOM

After spending the whole morning panicking and learning everything we could about doughnuts, we'd had the tables turned on us.

If I wasn't a fan of doughnuts before, now I was surely coming to hate the stupid little deep-fried assholes.

I exchanged a look with Wren, but I couldn't read him, although it wasn't hard to guess that he was panicking in equal measure.

Behind us I saw Amy twist her braided hair around her fingers, and Phil kept looking at the bleachers where a sweet-looking woman, likely his wife, was waving, unaware of what was happening.

Bea had a smile on her face and looked excited to start the challenge. Maybe she'd made these doughnuts before. Sadly, she was too far away for me to take any sneaky peaks at her work.

"Good afternoon, ladies and gentlemen," the contest presenter announced. "Thank you all for being here. I would like to apologize publicly to our brave contestants on behalf of the organization for the last-minute change, but would also like to thank you for coming back for this round."

He raised his hands to encourage a round of applause from the audience. There were still plenty of people on both sides of the bleachers considering the change. Word got around in small towns, and it looked like Chester Falls was no different.

"Now, ladies and gentlemen, there is an additional challenge to this round. As you know, our amateur bakers have the opportunity to practice for their bakes between rounds, but on this occasion, we've had to change the recipe to allow them to complete the challenge."

Some people in the audience booed and some whistled.

"Contestants, are you ready? You may commence."

I wanted to say I wasn't ready. I wanted to throw a tantrum, but then I remembered the ever-wise words of my idol: *since everything is in our heads, we had better not lose them.*

She was right. I'd baked a cake and cupcakes before. The difference with the doughnuts was that they were deep fried, but in essence they were like a cake.

I took a deep breath and counted to twenty, just to be doubly calm, and focused on the beat of my heart. Then I opened my eyes and started reading the recipe again.

Each step of making the batter was easier than I'd originally expected. This one didn't need proofing so I kneaded it, rolled it out, and used the cutters to get the right ring shape.

The deep fryer was scary to work out. I was terrified I'd get burned. When the little green light appeared I knew the temperature was right, so using a funny spoon that had holes in it, I lowered each doughnut into the hot oil.

The recipe said to fry each doughnut for one minute and then turn it over. It was harder than I thought, so by the time I got to the last one it was a really dark shade of brown.

My hands were so sweaty that when I started removing the doughnuts from the oil I dropped the spoon in twice.

The hard part was done, so while I waited for the doughnuts to cool down I made the glaze to coat them.

I didn't dare look at Wren or any of the other contestants. I knew this was going to be a difficult one for us.

We all placed our plates on the judging table behind our names and then flipped the cards upside down so the judges wouldn't know who baked what.

I stole a glance at the other contestants' doughnuts and my heart fell when I realized mine were by far the darkest ones. I must have set the fryer on a really high temperature.

Bea walked past me with hers, which looked absolutely delicious. I followed to the locker room, went straight into one of the cubicles, and finally let the tears I'd wanted to shed all day flow freely.

"Tom?"

Wren's voice on the other side made it even worse and the silent tears became loud sobs. The door opened slowly, which was when I realized I hadn't even locked it when I'd come in.

Wren kneeled on the floor in front of me and held my hands.

"That was pretty hard, wasn't it?"

I nodded.

"Apart from Bea's all of them look pretty bad. Don't give up yet until we know who's going home." He ran his hands over mine in a soothing motion, but I didn't want to feel better, I wanted to win the competition.

"You don't understand, do you?" I said.

"Understand what?"

"I need this more than anyone. You already have everything

you want: the career, the life. I don't. I need this to work out or I'll be stuck forever in a job I'm way over-qualified to do."

The more I spoke the angrier I got, and deep down there was part of me that knew this wasn't Wren's fault, but he was the one who'd invited me to his place last night. He was the one who'd distracted me so much I'd forgotten about the proofed dough. I hadn't been able to practice the frying part of the challenge and it was his fault.

I walked out of the cubicle, only turning around to say, "I need some time to myself," and then I went over to the sink to wash my face of tears and build up the strength to deal with being booted off the competition.

We all stood in a row awaiting the results. There was a low murmur coming from the audience, and I wondered if they knew the challenge had gone so wrong for all of us. Or maybe they'd expected someone to set something on fire today and were disappointed that it hadn't happened.

"Ladies and gentleman, you may have noticed we are one contestant short for this announcement."

I looked around and true enough Bea wasn't with us. Where had she gone?"

"Unfortunately, it has come to our attention that one of our contestants is currently enrolled in a culinary school. As this is against the rules, we have had to exclude the contestant from further rounds. This means all four contestants with us right now will go through to the semi-final. Congratulations!"

The crowd got up and cheered. I picked up the next recipe from one of the organizers and left the gym.

I walked the two miles back to the town center, hoping to get my thoughts in place. By the time I got there both Bookmarked and Spilled Beans were closed.

My store still had the rental sign up. It had been almost

two weeks since I'd last been here. Working longer hours in the store and researching and practicing for the bake-off had filled my days and my head space.

Standing in front of the store I remembered again why I was doing it all. Why the long hours, why I hadn't stopped in months, why I was participating in a contest that did not involve any kind of fashion.

I'd bought a chaise longue in a yard sale months ago. It sat in the middle of my living room waiting to be restored. I'd looked up everything I needed to bring back the wooden structure to good condition and how to re-upholster the fabric.

When I'd seen that chair, it had spoken to me. I'd seen in my mind's eye the customer sitting with the cocktail glass in hand, waiting to see the wonderful clothes I'd chosen for them. The little kids who waited patiently for their mom or dad to be fitted with a new dress or suit, and they'd have a fancy glass of juice and some coloring pencils.

I'd wanted to bring Fabulize to Chester Falls. It was such a ridiculous name that I couldn't resist picking it because it was everything I was. Fabulous but not quite like the rest.

A tear ran down my face. I wanted Fabulize so much it physically hurt to see the store space empty.

I shivered in the cool evening and thought of Wren.

We hadn't even had a proper conversation about the meaning of what we were doing. I didn't want to get hurt, as it was I was already too fragile and didn't know if I could handle it.

"Okay, Tom. Deep breath. Re-focus," I said to myself.

I started walking home, planning in my head what I needed to do to win the competition, and it started by being a new Tom. I needed to be the Tom that went for it and created his own opportunities. The time to help others would come when I opened the store.

My cellphone buzzed in my pocket and I took it out to see a few messages from Indy and Wren. I replied to Indy's message to let him know I was through to the next round, but I couldn't even bear to look at Wren's.

I would see him tomorrow in the store, but I had the next twelve hours before I needed to face him.

WREN

I couldn't say I'd had a feeling about Bea, because I hadn't even exchanged a word with the girl, but I had thought it strange that when all the contestants had been friendly and supportive of one another, she'd kept to herself.

I'd put it down to her being a lot younger than the rest of us, or maybe shy, but now I knew it was something else altogether.

The whole situation brought back memories of Zack's cheating. As a kid I'd been upset that I was being accused of something I hadn't done. My parents had always encouraged me to be truthful and true to myself, but I hadn't even known about Zack cheating on the test, let alone tell on him.

When I'd come home for the holidays on my first year of college, I'd bumped into him. He'd been working at the gas station outside of town. The boy that I'd played football with had grown older than his years, and I'd felt sorry for him and guilty that I'd taken his place.

I'd talked to my mom about it afterward and she gave me some really precious advice. If I'd earned my place in the team then I hadn't taken it from someone else. It simply meant that

I'd worked hard enough that when the position opened I was the first person in line for it.

The responsibility for the opening of the position lay solely with Zack. He was the one that made the decision to do something he knew could jeopardize his place in the team. Yes, there was misplaced anger, but after a while she'd assured me that Zack was probably angrier with himself.

I'd thought about it but kept coming back to the why. Why had he done it to start with? And it wasn't until I'd seen him with his family that I'd understood. Even though we weren't wealthy by any means, my parents both had a secure job in the store. Football was Zack's way out of an uncertain future, and when the stakes are that high people can do stupid things and risk losing it all on the off-chance they might make it.

Was Bea like Zack? She hadn't been cocky or arrogant. She'd done a good job with her bakes and kept to herself. Maybe this had been her high-stakes situation and like Zack it had cost her.

And how about Tom? His words in the cubicle had cut right through me and into my heart. He wasn't downright accusing me, but it really felt like it.

I knew it hadn't been my fault. We'd both practiced the challenge together and we had both become distracted with each other. We'd even received the notification of the date change at the same time. Deep down I knew he knew that, and that he'd just been upset about how badly the challenge had gone, but I hadn't expected him to react to me that strongly.

I'd come home feeling like I'd been stomped on my chest so hard I couldn't even feel anything anymore.

As I put the key in the door of my parents' apartment above the garage I laughed to myself. My teammates had always joked about the fact I was hard to read unless people were let in to my cues. They'd called me the iceman, first a joke but then it had stuck when sports commentators had picked up on it.

Only we'd known how far from being cold I was with my team, but we'd had a job to do on the field.

As I closed the door behind me and saw the ruined dough still in the bowl on top of the counter, I knew the iceman had to come back. It may be the only way to protect my heart and have a chance at winning the competition for my parents.

~

The next two days were spent in my parents' kitchen practicing for the semi-final under the supervision of my dad and Troy.

My dad was making a good recovery, and while we knew it was going to be slow, he was already walking farther and farther each day.

My mom had insisted I needed some time off from the store. Between the long hours and the competition, I hadn't actually had much time to do what I'd come to Chester Falls to do. Spend time with my family, particularly my dad.

It was just what I needed to help me focus, so by the time I stepped into the high school gym I was feeling confident and calm. Troy and my dad were in the bleachers right at the front cheering for me.

Before coming I'd wondered if we'd have a full station each, since there were less of us now, but my hopes were crushed when I saw two rows only, and I would have bet my life on sharing my station with Tom as before.

He didn't turn up until the challenge was about to start.

My heart beat out of my chest as Tom approached our station looking as confident as I'd ever seen him. He waved at the bleachers and I saw Indy and Ellie smiling and waving back, giving him the thumbs up.

When he came closer I saw something in his eyes: a challenge. It was then that I noticed what he was wearing. The same painted-on white jeans he'd had the other week that left no room for imagination, not that I needed it now that I knew what Tom looked like under his clothes, how soft his skin was, or how he got goosebumps whenever I licked just under his belly button.

He also had a crop top, but this one was a little shorter while also showing a lot more of his shoulder.

I remembered kissing that soft skin, and how Tom had melted under my touch. We'd fit so perfectly together, his smaller body against mine, like I was made to keep him warm, safe.

The tiniest chuckle came from the other side of the station. Tom knew exactly what he was doing to me.

This challenge was going to be an exercise in self-restraint. If I made it to the end of this without pulling Tom into the locker room and having my way with him. And that made me angrier with myself than anything else, because even after everything I still wanted him.

If I was to get through this challenge I'd need to be so cool that if someone looked up the word iceman they'd find a picture of me.

"Here we are again, ladies and gentlemen. Our four contestants have been practicing hard and the grocery store has run out of canned fruit." Everyone laughed at the joke. "We've had delicious chocolate fudge cake and beautiful rainbow cupcakes. Let's not go there with the doughnuts, but no one is more excited to see the upside-down cakes our bakers are attempting today. I shall be paying close attention to the making of my favorite ever cake."

When we were given the go-ahead to start I lined up all my ingredients. The hardest part of the cake was making the caramel that would go on the bottom of the cake tin. I'd had mixed results during my practice at home.

A glance at Tom, and he was lining his tin with butter. His movements were smooth and practiced, but it was the way his top showed his shoulder that had me struggling to look away. I wondered if I looked closer there would be any marks from when I sucked on his skin days ago.

The clearing of a throat got my attention, and I looked at the presenter, who was giving me a chiding look.

I went back to my own cake but it was hard to focus. Tom's presence next to me felt bigger than himself, and I was aware of every single movement next to me.

My first two tries at the caramel burned. The third was good enough, but I was running out of time, so I placed the fruit on top of the caramel and then moved on to the batter.

There was nothing to do while we waited for the cakes to bake, so we were given the option to sit with our supporters so we could keep an eye on our ovens.

Troy and my dad made room for me between them. I let out a relieved breath as I sat down.

"It looked really tense out there," Troy said.

"Try doing something you've never done before in front of an audience," I joked as I elbowed him.

"How do you think you did, Son?" my dad asked.

I pursed my lips. "Don't know, Dad. I guess I'll find out when I flip the cake out onto the plate."

Tom sat with Indy and Ellie on the opposite side of the gym. He was gesticulating like he always did when he was talking about something he cared about. The smile on his face was genuine, open, unlike the smile he'd given me earlier.

What would it take to have him smile like that at me

again? My stomach tightened as his gaze met mine across the hall. He froze for a second before he looked at Troy and my dad and waved at them.

"I really don't know how Tom gets away with wearing those clothes, but they look great on him," Troy said.

"You gotta own it, Son. Be your own individual," my dad said, and then he put his hand on my leg.

My throat felt like it had something trapped in it. Was my dad trying to say something with his comment?

The oven timers all went off all within seconds of each other, so we all went back to check on the cakes. Mine looked done, so I took it out and put the tin on the cooling rack. We had to wait a little longer for the cakes to cool down enough to be turned over, and that's when we'd know if we'd done well or not.

God, how had I played football in front of thousands of people before and was reduced to a pile of nerves over a cake?

TOM

After the wreck of the last challenge, I was walking on cloud nine with my upside-down cake. Every step had gone exactly how I'd practiced; now all I could do was wait and pray the cake would turn out perfect.

"Are you going to tell us exactly what's up with you?" Indy said.

"I really don't know what you're talking about."

"Really? I find that hard to believe," Ellie said, tickling my exposed shoulder.

I had my game plan going and from Wren's reaction it was working. He'd nearly dropped his mixing bowl twice, and I totally heard him groan when I bent over to pick up a spoon that had tragically fallen on the floor.

"Sometimes a girl has to pick herself off the floor and dust it off," I said just as my timer went off. "Time to check on my baby."

I saw the look they exchanged as I got up, but I couldn't tell them what was going on.

The main reason I never hooked up with guys in the closet

was because I didn't feel comfortable talking about them behind their backs, whether my friends knew them or not.

With Wren there was an added layer of complication because not only did my friends know him, I'd also come to really care for and respect his parents. Wren had the right to come out to them when he was ready, so even though I wanted to talk to my friends about how I was feeling, I knew I couldn't.

After the cakes were sufficiently cool it was time to turn them over onto a plate. I crossed my fingers and said a little prayer for it to come out nicely.

The smell alone had my mouth watering. I picked off the parchment paper carefully to make sure it didn't stick to the pineapple. Once it was all off I couldn't help letting out a relieved chuckle.

My cake was absolutely perfect. The caramel had a delicious shade of dark amber, and I could see the cake was cooked through even with the moisture from the fruit.

I looked at Wren and his expression was one of defeat. His cake was slightly burned on the top even though the parchment had come off completely. Amy was as happy with her cake as I was with mine, and I looked behind me to see Phil with his head on his hands and half a cake on the plate.

Amy shrugged when our eyes met. Phil's cake was half stuck to the tin.

Wren stared at his cake as if he was willing it to unburn. I wanted to tell him his wasn't as bad as Phil's, but the words couldn't leave my mouth. We hadn't spoken since the last challenge, and I hadn't even seen him in the store.

He looked at me and my cake and then picked his up to take it to the judging table and then left toward the locker room. I did the same.

I found Wren sitting at the back of the room facing the

lockers away from the door. His arms were crossed and he was staring ahead like he was lost.

"Wow, Tom, your cake looks so good," Amy said, picking a plate of food from the table.

"How can you eat? My stomach is in knots," I said.

"I feel so sick before these challenges I can't eat, but as soon as it's over and I can't control the outcome it's like a well opens. What I'd die for right now is a slice of your cake, honestly, it looks so delicious I think you won't have any problems going to the final."

At the other end I saw Wren's shoulders tense up. What was wrong with him? Hadn't he seen Phil's cake? Surely Phil wouldn't go to the final after presenting a cake that was half in the baking pan.

We were called out to get the results. Amy held my hand and smiled. She was really nice, and I hoped after this we could meet up for a coffee and be friends.

As soon as the results were announced Wren bolted while I went to meet my friends on the bleachers. Indy caught me winking back at Wren after he sent me an angry look. I wasn't even sure why he was angry with me when we'd both gone through to the final.

"Don't play with fire, Tom. You'll get singed."

"Or maybe I'll get burned and it'll be twice the fun," I teased.

Jonas and Troy came over on their way out to congratulate me.

"I hope you understand this means you have to bake for us in the store," Jonas said.

I laughed. "Is that with the approval of the boss?"

He gave me a strained look. "She has me on rabbit food these days. *And* she found all my jelly bean hiding places. I have no life anymore."

"Careful, Jonas, you're sounding as dramatic as me when I don't get my way."

"You haven't seen the half of it," Troy said.

I smiled as they walked out of the hall. Phil sat with his wife, who was consoling him.

"Hey, Phil. Sorry it's the end of the road for you," I said.

"I'm kind of relieved to be honest. I wanted the prize money to take Janet on a cruise, but I've been so stressed. I figured putting in more hours at work would earn me the same money even if it took a little longer."

"That's the spirit. I hope you get to your cruise soon."

I left them and joined Indy, who was giving us all a ride back into town.

My first job when I got home was to wash up the mess I'd made practicing my cake. Once that was done I got in the shower and let the stress of the day wash over me. I even used my favorite sparkly soap and cleaned extra thoroughly.

My cock perked up while I was cleaning myself off, but my stomach won that battle, so I got out of the shower and settled in front of the TV with a slice of cake after putting on some old T-shirt and sweatpants.

I was jolted awake by a knock on the door. The sky outside was dark. I looked at the clock on the wall and saw it was already past ten in the evening.

The knock became more insistent, and in my groggy state I opened the door without thinking.

"Wren?"

"You didn't ask who it was."

"What?"

"You can't just open the door without asking who's on the other side."

I didn't know what to say to that, but I went from half-asleep and confused to wide-awake and confused.

"Only residents have a key to the front door of the building. How did you get in?"

"I had a late delivery to one of your neighbors."

I crossed my arms and waited for him to tell me what the hell he was doing knocking on my door. He scanned me up and down, his eyes darker than I'd seen them before.

"What do you want, Wren?"

He ran his hands through his hair and let out a frustrated groan.

"Can I come in, please?"

I stepped aside. I smelled his soap as he walked past. My cock twitched in my underwear from the memory of the last time we were together.

"Why did you do it?" he asked. His voice bitter.

"Do what?"

He walked toward me but stopped at arm's length.

"You know what." His voice was low and deep and it went straight to the right places. I bit my lower lip and then soothed it by passing my tongue over it.

Wren's eyes tracked my every movement.

"You picked that outfit to make a point. You didn't just throw it on, did you?"

The tone of his voice was accusatory, which put my back up straight away, even though I knew he was right.

"I make no secret that I love fashion and I was feeling confident about the challenge so I dressed accordingly." There. That was a good argument. Right?

He stared at me. The silence was like a third person in my small apartment. I was about to give in and apologize when Wren spoke again.

"Do you know why I'm in the competition?"

I shook my head.

"Because Mason's is struggling financially. Because my

parents need a goddamned break, and because they're one unexpected expense away from having to let you go."

My stomach sank all the way down to the ground and into the apartment beneath mine. Hell, it was six-feet under with how stupid I felt.

"I had no idea, Wren."

He walked toward the window and looked out.

"I don't want to fight with you," he said, rubbing his short scruff.

My whole being wanted to be with Wren, touch him, comfort him, and do all the things that made the damned glitter snow globe in my belly shake.

I shook my head. My body was coiled tight in anticipation as I took two steps closer. Even from the short distance I felt Wren's body radiating heat.

He turned around and his eyes went from sad and doubtful to warm and hopeful.

We both moved at the same time, our mouths clashing together in a war for dominance. Wren picked me up and I wrapped my legs around him while I gripped his short hair. He groaned when I tightened my hold on him and I took the chance to plunge my tongue into his mouth.

"Tom." He groaned as he put his mouth on my neck and sucked so hard I knew I'd get an instant hickey.

My cock was as hard as a fucking rock, and I felt his against my stomach. "Fuck." I wanted him so badly I couldn't even articulate.

"Where's your bedroom?"

His eyes were lustful, dark pools of need. I nodded toward the end of the hall and kissed him again. He was strong enough to carry me, so I got busy undoing the buttons on his shirt. He put me on the floor and I finished opening his shirt and went straight for his jeans.

I palmed the outline of his cock and looked up to see him staring at me.

"Did you know I could see your jock strap through those fucking jeans?" He shrugged the shirt off and pulled my T-shirt out. "You picked that top because you knew I'd think of nothing else but your soft skin."

He bent down to take my nipple into his mouth, so I pushed him onto my bed and straddled him.

"That's better," I panted.

His hands went straight to my ass as his mouth turned my nipples into sensitive peaks. He pulled my sweatpants and underwear down, leaving them trapped just over my knees, and wrapped his hand around my already-leaking cock.

"Honest to god, Wren, if this doesn't end up with you balls deep inside me I'm going to kill you."

He chuckled. "Is that what you want?"

I put my hands on his face and tilted it up. My hungry mouth met his as I pushed him again so he was lying down. I snaked my way down his body to remove his pants and mine. As I moved back up I kissed every inch of his thick muscly thighs until I reached my prize.

"You have the best fucking cock I've ever seen." I gave it a slow stroke before I lowered my mouth onto the crown and sucked hard.

Wren cursed and I took more of him deeper into my throat, making sure to stop before it was too late.

"You're such a fucking tease," he said as he turned us over and placed his heavy body on top of mine, grinding our cocks together.

I let out a noise that was something between a contented sigh and a frustrated moan.

"Please, Coco, I don't need to eat or sleep, just keep his body like this on top of mine forever."

"Wish granted," he said, and I opened my eyes wide.

"Did I say that out loud?"

"Uh huh."

"Then keep my mouth busy before I say more stupid stuff."

"Your mouth will be plenty busy, baby, but I want to hear all your stupid stuff."

Right then in that moment I lost a little piece of my heart to Wren and was pretty sure the rest would follow soon, so I did as Tom does.

"Are you going to fuck me already or what?"

WREN

"*P*atience," I said, leaning back on my knees. My cock stood painfully hard, so I stroked it, putting on a show for Tom. "When you turned up wearing those jeans I nearly came on the spot."

"You liked what you saw, huh?" he said, biting his lip as he turned around and arched his back to give me the best view of his ass.

"Do you know what happens when I get riled up?" I lifted his hips up, which gave me a better view of his eager little hole.

Tom reached out for my hand and sucked on a finger, closing his eyes as if he was doing it to my cock. He may as well been for how much I was leaking.

"Hmm, show me..." He released my finger with a pop and lowered my hand down to his ass.

I circled his rim, adding a little bit of pressure. Tom closed his eyes and let out a moan.

"Where's your lube?" I asked.

He gave me a devious smile and pointed to the bedside table.

"Are you hiding any toys in there, Tom?"

"Not exactly hiding when I'm telling you where they are."

I opened the drawer and gasped when I found a range of butt plugs of different sizes. I pulled out the lube and picked a small plug.

He chuckled. "Interesting choice."

I raised an eyebrow.

"I was wearing that one the first day you saw the jeans."

My eyes went from the plug to Tom's ass to his face. "But you were wearing a jockstrap."

It was his turn to raise a brow. "You were looking, were you?"

"Baby, your ass was in front of my face all day wearing a glue-on pair of white jeans. But I never thought you'd be wearing a plug."

Fuck, could I be any more turned on by this man? I got off the bed to take a condom from my wallet.

"You're a boy scout," he said, stroking his cock slowly and putting on his own show.

"Nope, but I've wanted you since your first words to me were the name of the cologne I was wearing. I will always be ready for you."

I lubed up the plug and lined it up with Tom's hole, and then I covered his body with mine, kissing him as I pushed the plug in. I wanted to take in every breath, every moan out of this man as I filled him up.

"That's it, baby, take it all in. Stretch your sweet tight hole so you can take me all in one go."

His body trembled beneath me. His hands were wrapped tight around my back as if he never wanted to let me go. I already knew how it would be when it was me inside him, and I couldn't wait to feel his tight heat around my cock.

"One day, I want you *and* the plug in me."

I would have come on the spot from his words if I hadn't been so focused on him that I'd neglected my own cock.

Five seconds was all it took for me to put the condom on and add a little more lube to it. His hole twitched when I took the plug out, and he let out a little moan of frustration.

"Shh, baby. It'll be okay soon."

Despite my promise to take him in one go, I'd been afraid to hurt him. He was incredibly tight and my dick wasn't the smallest. He felt incredible around me, so hot, tight, perfect.

"Fuck, Tom...are you okay? Can I move?"

"Please, please."

I'd been with a few men, and some had even been short relationships that had gone nowhere, but moving inside Tom, feeling his legs wrap around me as he tried to match my thrusts in an attempt to take more, was unlike anything else I'd experienced before.

"I want to ride you," he said.

I grabbed his waist and without leaving his tight heat I moved us so I was almost sitting up on the bed with Tom on top of me.

His cock was hard and a deep red. I knew if I touched him he'd come in no time at all. He put his hands on my shoulders and raised himself before he came back down.

The feeling was overwhelming. Tom was taking charge and I loved every single bit of it. He set the pace, which was relentless. I knew every time my cock hit his prostate because he let out little whimpers as though he was in pain, and his eyes almost rolled back. His lips were red from how he was biting on them.

I pulled him to me and straightened up so his cock was trapped.

"You're ready to come aren't you, baby?"

He shook his head and never stopped thrusting his hips. His movements were a little less precise. He had to be close.

"Tom, baby, I'm ready to come, come with me. Please."

"I want it to last." There was a desperation in his voice I hadn't heard before.

My hands cradled his face and he opened his eyes to look at me.

"Baby, we can do it again."

I kissed him hard, and with every time he came down on my cock I tightened my arms around his waist to keep him there. My orgasm hit me like a tackle on the football field, and I unloaded into the condom. Tom came straight after me in a full-body orgasm that had him shake relentlessly as he covered us in his release.

Everything was quiet for a couple of minutes other than our mingled breaths as we recovered from our orgasm, but we refused to stop kissing.

"Can we have a shower?" I asked.

He nodded but didn't make an effort to move.

I picked him up and took him to his bathroom. He stood leaning against the sink while I turned the water on and disposed of the condom.

It wasn't until I was lathering him in the glittery soap I'd heard him mention before that he spoke.

"You have a magic cock. Can I keep it?"

"Tell you what, swap my magic cock with your magic hole and we have ourselves a deal."

He leaned against me, and I could tell he was struggling to stay awake.

"Can I stay the night?"

He nodded.

I got us out of the shower and dried us both using his plush towel, and then I led him to his bed, settling with him against me. He was asleep in seconds, and I drifted off shortly after.

A strong grip on my cock woke me from my sleep. I thought I was dreaming, but it seemed real life was giving me a hand job.

"What are you doing?" I asked.

"Go to sleep, I'm playing with my cock," Tom said.

"Your cock?"

"Hey, I was orgasm drunk, but I remember you said your magic cock was mine."

I chuckled. "How come you're awake?"

"I had a nap before you turned up, so I guess I'm not tired anymore."

The clock showed it was three in the morning, so we'd had a few hours' sleep already.

"Can I ask you a question?" I said.

"Sure. Do I need to stop playing with your cock to answer it?"

"Not unless want me to actually listen to you."

He put his hand on my chest and I held it, reaching out for a kiss.

"Will you tell me about the photo on the window display?"

"Sure. It's a photo of me and my dads when I was one year old."

"You have two dads?"

"Not anymore. They were in a car accident when I was two and a half. One of my dads died right away and the other weeks later in the hospital."

"I'm so sorry. Did you go into foster care?"

"No, my mom kept me. She's really my aunt because my non-biological dad was her brother, but she gave birth to me, and she's all I have, so to me she's my mom."

"Where is she?"

"Colorado. We lived in Boston since I was little, but when I moved out she decided she was tired of the city and went to live near her best friend."

I held him a little tighter because I didn't know what to say, but I wanted him to know I was there for him.

"Tom?"

"Yes?"

"Will you tell me more about your store?"

He sat up, and for a moment I thought he was upset, but he simply crossed his legs and faced me.

"There have been many times when I've had to blend in, play the game. We can argue that no one should have to do that, but sometimes we need to go through those stages where we are like everybody else, so that one day we can stand on our own two feet and become the individuals we are."

His words spoke to me as if he was inside my mind and had found the playbook of my life. My chest was tight and heavy with the weight of my secret, but Tom didn't seem to notice because he carried on.

"I want to paint one of the walls black and then hang photos of Coco Chanel. She's my idol and my muse, did I ever tell you?"

Tom's whole body lit up as he talked about the store. He was so passionate about his dream I felt a little jealous. When was the last time I felt like that about anything? I didn't want to dwell on it, not when my time was better spent admiring Tom.

"How would you make me look better?" I asked, tickling his sides. His giggles brightened up the dark room and all I wanted was to bottle them up to take with me everywhere.

He slapped my hand away and then put a finger over his mouth as if he was considering what to do with me.

"I think you'd fill out a tailored suit perfectly. Light gray, because bulge, and a waistcoat. Shirt rolled up to show your forearms...hmm yummy."

With every pass of his eyes over my body my skin heated up and my cock reacted accordingly. I pulled him down and he lined his body up with mine and nuzzled his head in the crook of my neck. "You are so beautifully amazing. I am really glad we met...even if that threat of arson is still over my head."

His chest rumbled against mine. "I'm keeping that one in my pocket."

"You're naked," I said, pulling his leg over mine to get him closer.

"Proverbial pocket."

"You would have one."

"I would." He laughed.

TOM

There was something about Wren asking about my photo that spoke right to my heart. I'd seen the day I'd finished the window that he knew the photo was personal.

Yes, it was a tragic story and some days I thought about my dads and wondered what it would have been like to have come home from school as a teenager, trying to figure out my sexuality and being able to talk to them. Not that my mom wasn't good with that. She'd been absolutely brilliant, but it wasn't the same.

The purpose of using the photo hadn't been to draw attention to my story, and as far as I was aware, no one knew the photo was mine. I just wanted to have something in the window that was really real. A couple that had a regular life, regular job, regular kid, they'd even had a regular death, the only different thing about them was that they were two men.

My mom had told me they hadn't joined in any of the LGBTQ activist events. They were, in her words, the most boring couple she'd ever known, and she even said I must have more of her DNA in me than that of my dad because I'd been anything but boring growing up.

So yeah, the photo meant a lot, and Wren asking about it gave me the opportunity to talk about my parents, something I didn't do much.

I hadn't expected the question about the store, but I was happy to share more of my dream. To be honest, lying in my bed in the dark of the night with Wren's arms around me, I would have confessed to anything, so talking about my passion for fashion and changing people's lives through it was the easiest thing I could do.

"Can I confess something?" Wren said.

"Of course."

"This is going to sound like a long-winded explanation but...listening to you talk about your store. I don't know, maybe I need to tell someone."

"You can tell me anything, sweetie," I said.

He was quiet for a mere second before saying in one breath, "I don't play football anymore."

There was a strain in Wren's voice. I wanted to show my support, so I stayed as we were cuddled together with me playing with the hairs on his chest.

"I had an injury a couple of years ago. After the surgery on my knee I had a long recovery ahead, but I'd always thought I'd get back on to the field. Until the doctor said that if I didn't want to risk permanent damage I'd retire. He also said I wouldn't ever be as fast as before. It felt like a death sentence. Football was all I had and the only thing that made sense. I couldn't tell my parents, not because they wouldn't understand, but because I didn't know who I was without it, and I didn't want to burden them."

I wrapped my arms tight around him because I could tell this was a big thing. Had he ever said these words to anyone before? There was no doubt his parents would be fully supportive but maybe being so far away from home made it harder.

"I'm so, so sorry, Wren. I don't even know what to say to make you feel better." Was there anything anyone could say? Oh my sweet Wren.

Wren's hand came up to my head and he played with my hair. It was soothing and so natural, like we'd been having late-night deep conversations since the dawn of time.

He took a breath and carried on.

"I received a small settlement for my injury, which allowed me to buy my apartment and retrain as a teacher. I work in a high school in San Diego as the football coach and physical education teacher."

"Do you like it?"

"Surprisingly, I love it. The kids are great and I can pass on all the stuff I learned over the years. For the first time in my life I feel like I'm myself. I'm out at work and have great friends who think because I'm bi I need to date every single person we meet in a bar."

I liked that Wren was so open about his life in San Diego, and I knew he'd just confessed something really major, but there was an ugly gremlin inside me that didn't want him to have a great life in San Diego, didn't want to know of all the potential people he could be dating as soon as he went back.

A pain cut through my chest so hard I had to cough and sit up in bed. He was going in less than a week. I wasn't sure of the actual day, but Abi had mentioned something about the end of the bake-off.

My eyes stung and I was so thankful that we were in the dark because it was easier to pretend my thoughts weren't upsetting me, so I did what Tom does. Deflect.

"Are you telling me your sob story so I fall asleep and you don't have to tell me why you're my forever bake-off rival?"

He laughed and kissed my head as soon as I resumed my position.

"When I got the news about my dad I didn't think twice about coming home. It's been a while since I was here and I missed it. I wanted to take the chance to speak to my parents too and tell them the truth, but then when I got to the store and saw their accounts my priorities changed."

"I still don't understand how the store is struggling. We're always so busy."

"The store is doing well, but they've had a few expenses, and I think they've also spent some money on really expensive equipment for Troy. I wish they'd asked for help because I could have bought some of the stuff. But anyway, it means the store needs to keep bringing the same level of income just to stay afloat, and if a big expense comes along they could be in real trouble."

"Wren?"

"Yes, baby?"

"We both have really good reasons to be in the bake-off. Can we just put the result in the judges' hands? I don't want to fight with you. Whoever wins the prize deserves it whole-heartedly. And I'm sorry about how I behaved the other day. I didn't mean to accuse you of anything, I know it wasn't your fault. I was just so scared I hadn't done enough to go through."

"That's okay, I knew you how you felt because I was feeling the same. I'm not sorry for your revenge though," he said, running a blunt nail from the back of my knee and up my thigh until his hands settled on my ass.

"No?"

"I'm pretty sure I came out the winner."

Wren moved so he was on top of me. I gasped when I felt his hard cock against my hardening dick.

"Are you going to let me play with your magic dick again?"

"You bet I am."

Despite the looming bake-off final and Wren's departure, I'd never felt as happy. Okay, so maybe I was ignoring the fact that we had three challenges to do on the day and we had no clue what they were, but because I couldn't control it, I decided to not worry about it.

And the same went for Wren's departure. He hadn't talked about it at all, almost as though he didn't want to say when he was going in case it happened. And so I hadn't pushed.

Ignorance was bliss, as they say.

Wren had spent all of his free time with me, including the nights. Abi had asked if I'd heard anything about him seeing someone because he hadn't been home for days. I pleaded ignorance.

Abi was starting to come back to herself since the day of Jonas's heart attack, and I knew part of it was because Jonas was recovering well, and part of it was because she held hope that this *person* Wren was supposedly seeing was important enough for him to stay home.

I didn't want to break her heart by telling her it was unlikely. I had my own hopes.

The gym was full to the brim with people coming to watch the final. Amy came to me as soon as I walked in.

"Oh my god, I'm so nervous I think I'm going to puke."

"Stay away from me, woman. This outfit does not do well with body fluids."

I ran my hands down my new turquoise vest I'd made only last night as Wren had watched TV on my sofa. He'd looked so comfortable there, like he belonged in my space.

He was driving with his parents, so I took my place at my station, noticing that for the final we each had our own.

I looked around and saw Indy, Ellie, Hannah, and Ben waving. Ellie had a banner with my name on it in glitter. It was fabulous. I waved at them and made a heart sign with my hands.

Wren smiled and winked as he walked past me on the way to his station. I felt like I was hovering, feet off the ground, with happiness.

When we were given the sign to start I looked at the recipes we needed to make. A chocolate mousse, an apple pie, and a chocolate chip cookie. I figured the trick was in the timing. The mousse needed to set so I started with that.

It was a simple recipe, but I was afraid the whipped egg whites would end up all flat, so I was super careful when I blended them in the chocolate mix.

Once the mousse was in the individual ramekins and in the fridge, I decided to make the cookie as that wouldn't take long. It was a tiny recipe just for one big cookie that I had to cook in a skillet.

I made the mix and put it alongside the mousse in the small fridge I had on the counter.

Then I moved on to the apple pie. I was feeling confident so far. Nothing had gone wrong yet, and one challenge was complete, pending cooling.

I read through the recipe for the pie and that's when I realized my mistake. I needed to make the pastry and it needed chilling. No point thinking about it. I'd cook the cookie while the dough was chilling.

Three hours later and all three challenges were complete. Amy was in the station in front of me looking like she'd been in a war. I looked at Wren behind me and he wasn't faring any better.

We placed our desserts in front of our names for the last time and flipped the cards upside down before going back to the locker room.

"I'm so glad this is over," Amy said. "Don't even care who wins anymore."

"Not unless you do win. Your pie looked so delicious," I said.

Wren sat next to me on the bench. I had my arms crossed over my chest and my legs outstretched in front of me. Wren mimicked my position and then I felt his fingers brush over mine and stay there for a while.

I looked at him and it was then, as we shared such an intimate moment in a room with other people, that I knew I was falling for Wren Mason. Maybe already had. I looked down at my feet with a smile and a warmth on my cheeks.

Not long after, we were called back to find out who was the winner. My heart was beating so fast I struggled to hear the presenter's speech.

"And the winner of this year's Pride festival bake-off is... drum roll...Wren Mason!"

The crown cheered so loud it startled me. What did he say? Wren Mason. Wren had won. Happiness bloomed in my chest and I couldn't stop smiling. I looked at Wren and his parents and Troy were hugging and congratulating him.

I couldn't even get close to him because he was suddenly surrounded by the crowd of spectators, cheering and greeting him with hugs and high-fives. Everyone wanted Wren's attention.

His eyes were wide, like he couldn't believe it had happened. When everybody finally gave him some breathing space, I saw it as my opening to celebrate with him.

As I got near him I thought I felt him withdraw but put it down to him being overwhelmed with the attention. I reached out to touch his arm but he stepped back. He looked at me but his eyes were cold.

My heart sank as he shook his head to stop me and then turned the other way.

I ran out of the gym, not caring about seeing Indy, or any of my friends. I could barely see where I was going from the heavy tears in my eyes because I couldn't believe I'd fallen hook, line, and sinker for a man who rejected me at the first opportunity once he'd got what he wanted.

I just hoped no one had followed me because I didn't know what I'd say.

WREN

The first two hours after they announced me as the winner of the bake-off were a blur. I'd had to be interviewed for all the local papers and radio as well as take photos with the mayor, who wouldn't stop thanking me for the lack of major incidents this year, as though I was personally responsible for the other contestants. Then there were the people in town that wanted to congratulate me.

I'd had enough within about five minutes of the whole thing starting but needed to fulfill the role of the grateful winner. Not that I wasn't. Grateful, that is. I'd worked hard between the store and practicing for the challenges.

The one thing running like a loop through my mind was Tom's face when I'd reacted to him touching me. The shock, disappointment, and sadness. I needed to put it right.

My parents had gone home hours ago and so had Ellie, Hannah, Ben, and Indy. As soon as I was free from the bake-off obligations, I called a cab to take me to Tom's apartment.

I rang the bell but there was no answer. I rang again and again. One of his neighbors came in with some groceries, so I offered to help her to her door for an excuse to be let in.

She told me she'd seen Tom leave earlier in a cab, but she didn't know where he went. I knocked on his door, but after a while I accepted that he wasn't going to answer or he really was gone.

My first stop after that was Spilled Beans.

"Hey, Indy, have you seen Tom?"

"Hey, congrats, man. Sorry we couldn't stay earlier but had to come back to business."

"That's okay, I really just wanted to speak to Tom. Have you seen him?"

Indy narrowed his eyes. "I saw him leave the gym but thought he might have gone out for some fresh air before doing the whole award thing. Haven't seen him since."

"Can you let me know if you see him, I really need to talk to him."

I wrote my number down on a piece of paper, put it on the counter, and ran over the square to Bookmarked.

As soon as I walked in I knew both Ben and Ellie knew something because they looked at each other and then back at me with fake smiles.

"Do you know where he is?"

"Maybe, but why should we tell you?" Ellie said.

"Did he tell you why he's gone?"

Ellie blushed and shook her head. "I figured he'd lost his job or something. Now that you're back maybe you don't need him."

"I need him more than he knows, more than even I knew. Please, I need to speak to him."

Ben looked at his cellphone and then back at me again.

"He left for an important reason, Wren. Why should we break his trust for you?"

I ran my hands over my face, feeling the scratchy scruff.

"Look, I want to tell you but I think he deserves to know

first, my family too. You both once had to keep secrets until you didn't anymore." I let my statement hang. After a few breaths they looked at each other with wide grins.

"He's at Aunt Gina's place," Ellie said. "She lives outside of Chester Falls. If you want my advice, leave him for a couple of days. Once he calms down he'll come home and then you can sweep him off his feet."

I didn't correct her as I left the store, hearing Ellie behind me squealing, "I'm going to be a bridesmaid!"

My next stop was home.

My parents were both in the kitchen. Dad helping Mom out chopping vegetables.

"Hey."

"Hey, Son. Are you all done with the interviews? Your mom is making your favorite for dinner."

"Did she promise you jelly beans?"

My dad looked at my mom, who looked really guilty.

"You mean there are no jelly beans?" he cried. "Damn, this is modern day slavery."

I laughed and my mom got up to give him a kiss.

"Where's Troy? I kinda have something I want to tell you all about."

"I'm here."

"Jeez, do you have super hearing or something?" I said.

"No. If I can hear Dad cry about jelly beans all the way from my room, I can hear that there's gossip I need to know about."

"Okay, so there's two things. I'm not sure which one to start with so I'll just get it out. I'm no longer playing professional football. I had an injury that basically was serious enough to bench me for life. I now work as a coach and physical education teacher in a high school in San Diego."

They all looked at each other, but it was my dad that spoke.

"Son, do you think we don't own a TV?"

"What?"

"Do you think we wouldn't follow the career of our son?"

My face heated up in shame. Of course they'd know. Just because they weren't into sports it didn't mean they'd lose interest in what I was doing.

"Why didn't you say anything?" I asked.

"Why didn't you?" my mom asked back.

"I'm sorry, I guess I hoped I'd get back to playing, and then I was ashamed that after all the years of practices and games I was nothing more than a high school teacher."

"How much respect does this town have for Coach and Mrs. Johnson?"

I shook my head and sighed, because my dad was so right.

"Touché, Dad."

"What's the other thing?" my mom asked.

"Erm, thing is...I..." My words were stuck in my throat. They were all looking at me expecting something, and for the first time in my life I was afraid my family wouldn't accept me for who I was. "I'm bisexual."

"Oh Jesus Christ, Son. You nearly gave me a heart attack," my mom said, holding onto my dad's arm. He was smiling and Troy was shaking his head.

"What?"

"Dude, I can't believe I came out before you."

"You're bi?"

"Girls? Thanks but no thanks. I'm full Kinsey six gay."

"Since when?" I asked.

"Really? That's the question you want to ask?"

I laughed and ruffled his hair.

"Duuude," Troy groaned.

I got up to give my mom and dad a hug. Why had it taken me so long to do this? I already felt lighter than ever just for letting them see the true me, no lies.

"So this means you're staying and going to make an honest man out of our Tom?" my dad said.

"How...how do you know?"

"Son, I had a heart attack, I'm not blind. And you two haven't exactly been discreet with his coming up to the apartment after work and not leaving till the morning."

"Jesus, a guy can't have any secrets around here."

"There's one secret left. Are you going back to San Diego?"

The truth was that I hadn't thought that far. All I knew was that I wanted Tom back. I needed to tell him how I felt about him, and that I was done hiding who I was.

If he wanted me and he wanted to live in Chester Falls then that's what we'd do. I had no doubt my apartment would sell quickly or I could rent it out for a regular income.

"Coach Johnson did say he was considering retiring," I said.

My mom put her hands over her mouth, a tear running down her cheek.

"Oh, Mom."

"I'm so proud of you, Wren. You've always worked so hard for all the things you've wanted. You deserve to be happy many times over. I'm so happy you're considering coming home, but make sure you make that decision for yourself."

"Thanks, Mom."

My dad shook my hand and gave me a pat on the back.

"Now, does anyone know how I'm going to get my prince charming? Because I've never swept anyone off their feet, and I know if there's anyone who deserves it it's Tom."

TOM

I'd lost track of time. Had it been two days since I left Chester Falls? A week? All I knew was that according to the positioning of the sun it was about time for Gina's daily "let's cheer up Tom" conversation. Okay, she had cocktails too, but I wasn't even in the mood to drink sugary sweet drinks, and that was saying a lot.

What would I do now? That was all I could think about. How could I go back to Mason's and work with Abi and Jonas knowing all the secrets about their son and not even being able to ask for news.

I'd also disappeared without notice. What were they thinking of me? No doubt my job was no longer mine, and that was another thing to worry about. I would need to start using the savings I'd put aside for the store just to pay the rent and bills.

More tears spilled from my eyes, so I hid my face in the pillow.

My stupid brain only wanted to think about Wren. The time when he'd been making the doughnuts while I'd read out the recipe to him, the time when he'd nearly broken one of his parents' picture frames in his apartment because he'd been so eager to get his mouth on me he'd stopped halfway down the small corridor to the bedroom and pushed me against the wall.

The ease in which he picked me up like I was feather-light and all his. The stolen moments in the storeroom between serving customers. How his touch made me feel special, wanted.

I felt like such a fool for believing it, trusting him. Why did my brain refuse to move on from Wren? Was my heart in such control? Stupid, stupid heart.

My Coco said once, *there is time for work, and a time for love. That leaves no other time.* What if there was a time for work, and a time for work? Surely there was no time for love. No time for heartbreak.

I grabbed my cellphone from the bedside table and dialed my mom's phone.

"Mom?"

"Tom, baby, oh I missed you so much. You haven't called in forever."

"I know, Mom. I'm sorry, I've been kinda busy."

"You work too hard, honey. How are things in your new town?"

"I'm calling because of that, actually. Erm, I was thinking of visiting with you for a little while."

There was a small gasp. "Is everything okay?"

"Yes, Mom, well, no, but I just want to spend some time with you."

"Any time you want, honey."

"Thanks, Mom."

Just hearing my mom's voice made me feel a little better. I got up and went to the window. Gina had a lovely long yard that faced onto a field. Suddenly I felt like going for a walk.

I put on a pair of jeans and a sweater and went downstairs.

"Hey, Gina, can I borrow Cosmo for a walk?" And as if she knew we were talking about her, Cosmo, Gina's extremely spoiled and bossy cat, came in from the living room, sauntering in like she owned the place.

"Hey, sweetie, you've come out. Are you feeling better?" Gina asked.

"No, but I can't stay in the room for the rest of my life."

She looked up from her cellphone and then looked outside. "I'd love to join you on the walk, but I really could do with a cup of coffee. Do you want one before we go?"

"Sure."

Cosmo jumped on my lap as Gina turned to the coffee machine.

"Hey, baby girl, aren't you looking gorgeous today?" I cooed.

She bumped her head against my hand, demanding that I scratch her neck. Cosmo's love for me had been at first sight. I'd visited for the weekend months ago when I'd needed to escape the ultra-romance vibrations happening at the apartment between Charlie and Kris, and as soon as I'd walked in the door it was as if she'd known of my love of all things Cosmo, like the cocktail.

"I think I need a cat like you, Cosmo. What do you say? Will you help me find a suitable candidate?"

She purred and carried on nuzzling against me.

I heard tires on gravel outside as Gina put a cup of strong black coffee in front of me.

"Who's that, Cosmo? Is that your daddy coming home from work early? Is it?"

I kissed her little cold wet nose.

"Oh my god, he's worse than I thought," the voice of my best friend declared from the archway between the corridor and kitchen.

"Charlie!"

I got up to hug my best friend. As soon as I was in his arms I started sobbing. He held me tight and let me cry for as long as I needed to.

"I'm sorry, I didn't mean to slobber all over you," I said.

Kris placed a kiss on Charlie's head and left us.

"Was he there all along?"

Charlie laughed. "Yes?"

I looked over at Kris before he turned to the living room.

"Damn that ass."

Charlie pinched my nipple.

"Hey! Okay, sorry. Are you sure he's safe with Gina?"

"Yeah, he has a whistle if she gets too close. So do you want to do this here or upstairs?"

"Do what?"

"Your pep talk."

I went over to the coffee maker and filled a mug for Charlie. He followed me upstairs without saying a word.

"So what's going on? Aunt Gina called worried about you. She said you haven't come out of your room in three days."

"Did you really come here from Lydovia to give me a pep talk?"

"Yup, now spill."

So I told my best friend about Jonas's heart attack, meeting Wren, the bake-off, our push-pull relationship, and how I ended up falling for a guy who was in the closet, and his reaction to me as soon as he'd won the money.

"Wow," Charlie said.

"I know."

"No, you don't. I mean, wow, is this how it feels?"

"I'm not following, Charlie. You want to start making sense?"

"When I called you to talk about Kris all those months

ago, and you had no second thoughts about telling me to go for it and be honest about my feelings. Is this how it feels?"

"I want to say your coffee is laced with something," I said. "But I poured it for you."

"Sweetie, did you tell him how you feel about him?" Charlie said with a soft smile.

"No."

"Is it possible that the way he reacted to you was a misunderstanding?"

My face heated up. Yes, okay, I had considered it, but I was being a brat and didn't want to think about it.

"Yes?"

"Then what are you doing here? Shouldn't you be having that conversation with him?"

My chest deflated like a sad balloon.

"He's probably already back in San Diego, living his old life. He said it himself, he likes it there and has friends out there. Not to mention he's out in San Diego, which means he's free to date whoever he wants."

"I'm going to take a wild guess here that he's not interested in anyone else, he hasn't gone back to San Diego, and that he feels exactly the same for you as you do for him."

"I don't know."

"What's the worst that can happen? Besides, if it doesn't work you can go to Colorado to lick your wounds at your mom's."

"Holy Coco, are there bugs in this room? How do you know?"

"The walls in this room are paper thin, Gina overheard you talk to your mom. Oh and by the way, when you find that I'm right and you get your guy, if you ever visit Gina, don't stay in this room."

It took me a while to get it, but when I did I burst out laughing.

Not long after Kris walked in the room. I was nearly crying with laughter.

"Please tell me she recorded it," I said as I tried to get my breath back.

They looked at each other.

"Noooooo."

"Yes," they both said.

"Gina is a legend."

Kris sat on the bed next to us and pulled Charlie into his arms. Charlie melted into him so fast I had to rescue the coffee mug.

"So, my adorable Tom Jones, what magic do you want me to weave so you can get your own prince?" Kris said.

"If you mean your bottomless credit card, then I think I just need a ride home. But if you fill up my fridge with champagne and buy me a bottle of Chanel Blue I'm not going to complain."

"Got it." He gave Charlie a kiss that even I felt and then left.

A mere hour later I was on the way home in Kris's very fancy hire car, sipping champagne, and holding a very large gift bag.

WREN

The best hundred dollars I spent in my life were undoubtedly on Tom's elderly neighbor who had no qualms about asking for compensation in exchange for calling me as soon as she saw Tom return. She also let me in the building for an extra twenty bucks. The woman drove a hard bargain, but I would have paid much more than that just to make sure I could see Tom again.

It had been a grueling three-day wait, but I'd made the best use of it by setting everything in motion. I just hoped it wouldn't blow up in my face.

I wore a pair of jeans I knew fit me really well and showed all the work I'd put in the gym and by running, and paired it with a navy V-neck long-sleeve shirt. Fall was in full force and soon winter would bring the freezing temperatures. It was already chilly enough in the evening that I couldn't be out without a coat.

So there I was, in front of Tom's door, dressed in my best outfit and holding a gift bag in one hand. I raised the other to knock at the same time as the door opened and Tom nearly crashed into me.

Our proximity reminded me of the first time we'd met, when I hadn't been able to form a coherent thought in front of the man that would eventually steal my heart.

"Hi."

"Hi."

"Erm, do you want to come in?" he asked.

I nodded and walked past him.

"Were you going somewhere? I don't want to keep you." I couldn't read his face. I wasn't sure if he was mad or upset with me.

"I was but I don't need to anymore."

"Oh, okay. Erm, I'm here because I need to apologize to you and explain my behavior after the competition."

Tom gestured for me to sit on his couch while he pulled the wooden coffee table back and sat on it. We were face-to-face, our knees nearly touching but not quite.

"When they announced me as the winner I didn't really pay attention, I thought they'd say your name so I wasn't expecting it. Everything happened so fast and then all these people ran to me to congratulate me. Tom, all I wanted to do was to shout that it was a mistake and they should give you the prize instead, but I couldn't see you in the sea of people.

"Someone pulled me and when I turned I saw Zack. I didn't recognize him at first but he threatened me, my family, and you unless I gave him the prize money."

Tom's face was one of shock. He shook his head.

"What did he threaten to do?"

"He didn't say at the time, there were too many people around, but I had a note on my car. It said he was going to set Mason's on fire and he'd make sure you had a taste of the real Chester Falls. He gave me twenty-four hours."

"Why me too? What did I do?"

"I don't know, the guy looked like he was on some kind of

drugs, but I didn't want to risk him thinking we were together. He was always known for his homophobic comments at school."

My heart raced as I told Tom what had happened after the competition as though it was happening again. He put his hands on mine and smiled.

"I'm okay, Wren. Nothing happened."

"They kept me there for so long taking photos and doing interviews. I knew you'd be safe because you were gone, but then..."

I squeezed his hands hard just to make sure he was there in front of me. Whether or not we still had a chance to be together, Tom was okay and that was all that mattered.

"What happened to him?"

"He was held by the police. They caught him driving under the influence and brought him to the station. By then I'd already spoken to the police chief and given him the letter and made a statement."

Tom squeezed my hand and I felt like I'd won the playoffs.

"I also came out to my family."

He looked surprised but had a proud smile on his beautiful face. I wanted to kiss him so badly.

"How did they take it?"

"I really underestimated my parents. They already knew about the football thing and were only a little disappointed that I didn't tell them myself."

"And how about the rest?"

"Did you know Troy is gay?" I asked.

"Yes."

"Well, I didn't, so first of all he made fun of me for coming out to our parents, and then my parents asked me about you."

"What?"

"It seems we weren't as discreet as we'd thought."

I cupped his cheek and he leaned into my touch.

"What exactly did you tell them about me?"

I sat back and pulled Tom forward so he didn't have a choice but to straddle me. He sat on my legs and put his hands on my chest.

"I told them that I'd fallen for you and I needed to find you so I could ask you to forgive me."

A large sob came from deep within Tom and he leaned forward, hiding his face on my chest.

"What's up, baby?"

"I have too. I've fallen for you so hard, I didn't know how to handle it when I thought you'd rejected me. I'm so sorry."

"Hey," I said, tilting his head up to face me. "Sounds like we're both suffering from the same affliction."

He smiled his bright Tom smile, his violet eyes shiny and his spark coming back.

"Oh yeah? What's that?"

"Well, if you can't feel mine, baby, then we have real problems."

As soon as his lips touched mine it was like a burst of color, light, and love growing from within and filling my chest with happiness.

The kiss soon became a heated battle. I groaned when Tom grabbed my hard dick through my jeans and moaned his appreciation. His mouth stole all my breaths until I wondered if I was going to pass out from so much pleasure, and we weren't even naked.

"Bedroom," I pleaded.

"You know what to do."

He was right, and if I had my way Tom would never need to walk to the bedroom ever again.

I'd also need to make sure there were no frames hanging on any hallway walls, but that was a talk for another day.

We kissed our way into the bedroom, our mouths hungry and passionate. Fuck, I'd never get tired of his mouth on mine.

"How did you get in the building, by the way?" Tom asked, kissing his way down my chest. He hovered over my nipples and looked at me.

There was a look of defiance in his eyes. My cock twitched in my pants in anticipation. He licked a nipple and then blew on it. A ripple of pleasure ran down my spine.

"Fuck, Tom."

"So...are you going to tell me how you got into my building?"

"I paid your neighbor."

He laughed. "Come again?"

There was another lick and cool breath over my other nipple. I raised my hips to meet Tom's, but he raised his too. I groaned my frustration.

"How much?"

"Hundred bucks. Can we get to the good part already?" I pleaded. I needed Tom's skin against mine.

"A hundred dollars?"

"And twenty for her to let me in, and I'd have paid double that, no scratch that, I'd have tripled that just to end up exactly where I am now."

"At my mercy?" he asked, finally lowering his hips and giving me a sliver of relief.

"Yes."

Tom sat back and removed his clothes in record time, only stopping to give me a look that was basically asking what the hell I was doing still dressed.

With both of us naked and wanting, all bets were off.

"By the way," Tom said as he tugged on my balls, causing me to hiss in pleasure. "We have gifts from Charlie and Kris so feel free to go all quarterback on me because we have supplies for a midnight snack and all the condoms in the world."

"Fuck yeah." I cheered.

It was the longest and shortest night of my life.

"Come on, baby," I said, dragging Tom by his hand.

I'd managed to keep this to myself last night when we'd talked, but I was bursting to tell him.

"Ugh, Wren, you can't expect me to be all sparkly when I've been up all night."

I stopped and turned around. He bumped into me and I wrapped my arms around him. I pushed his sunglasses up on his head.

"Baaabe." He pouted.

"Any regrets?" I said, sucking his bottom lip.

"None, but it doesn't mean I want to go all Mary Poppins around the town square."

I tucked him in the crook of my arm and walked us toward Bookmarked.

"I hope you know that by now Charlie told Connor, who told Hannah, who told Ellie, who told Ben, who told Indy that we're together."

"I'm counting on it."

Tom started steering us toward Bookmarked, but I pulled him over to the empty unit.

He tugged on my hand hard enough that I nearly crashed against him.

"Why did you stop?" I asked.

"I've come to terms with it that I'm not going to be able to rent it out, but it doesn't mean I want to look at it."

"Trust me?" I said and kissed him.

He nodded.

I held his hand and pulled him over to the store. I took the key from my pocket, opened the door, and led Tom inside. All the paperwork we needed was on the counter.

"What's happening, Wren?"

"Please don't be mad at me."

"What did you do?"

Tom's eyes were shiny and I knew he was trying to contain tears.

"You've earned this place, baby, so it's yours."

He shook his head like he couldn't believe it.

"Did you know there was a prize for the window competition?"

He shook his head again.

"Me either. There never used to be one. I mean, the prize was a trophy and the right to brag all year. Chester Falls has come a long way. Anyway, you won the window contest so you get the prize. Twenty thousand dollars."

Tom stared at me, his mouth open.

"I know it seems crazy, but the Pride festival is big here. What you've seen isn't even all of it yet. I guess there's more support and money in it so the prizes are bigger. Mom and Dad were really happy when I said I'd won the bake-off for them. It's given them a small cushion, but they wanted you to keep the prize for the window. You did it. You came up with the concept and you executed it."

"Is this real? I mean, it's my dream come true, but is it real?"

"You bet your cute little ass, that is now mine, that it is true."

TOM

Three months later

I wasn't sure which one was the happiest day of my life. The day that I first kissed Wren, the day he turned up at my door to make up, or when he told me he'd taken out a lease on my unit using the prize money from the window competition, leaving me with the rest for the furnishings and stock.

They were all great days, but today I was welcoming my friends and family for a pre-opening celebration in my dream store. I was finally the owner of my business.

My mom had come from Colorado last week and was loving Chester Falls so much I wouldn't be surprised if she left the mountains for the milder weather of Connecticut.

Charlie and Kris had flown in yesterday and this morning they were house hunting before attending the grand pre-opening event. When they'd said they had news I'd expected them to tell me they were engaged, but it was so much better than that because they were engaged with the cherry on top that they were looking for a home in Chester Falls so they didn't have to stay in Gina's playroom. Kris's words.

"Tom, honey?"

"Come in, Abi."

"Oh wow, sweetheart, it looks fabulous. I'm going to need your help picking an outfit. Jonas wants to take me to the theater in New Haven. It's our first date in years."

"Oh my god! Abi, I already have the perfect dress and accessories. Come by this week and I'll sort you out."

I hugged her tight. Abi and Jonas were brilliant to me. They'd let me carry on working in the store until I'd had too much work with the setup of Fabulize and needed to quit.

"Do you need me to convince Jonas to come along too?" I asked.

She winked and gave me a kiss.

"I'll see you later, honey."

One by one, my friends came in to see the store before the official opening. I couldn't wait to open tomorrow and welcome my first customers. Thanks to all the recommendations from the customers I'd met at Mason's, I already had a lot of bookings for personal styling.

I knew my net-a-porter range would also sell easily off the rack, especially ladieswear.

Behind the scenes I'd started designing my own collection inspired by none other than my muse, whose photo hung proudly on the wall just above the red chaise longue I'd painstakingly restored.

The clock was annoyingly slow when I checked it for the millionth time since this morning. I'd worked so hard in the last few weeks I'd barely spent any time with Wren, and then he'd had to go back to San Diego to complete the sale of his apartment.

We'd talked about moving in together when he came back, and I couldn't wait to have him in my bed every night. Well, he already was, since we'd either sleep at my place or his parents' apartment, but it was exhausting having to always plan where to have our food and which laundry needed doing.

Last week before he'd gone to San Diego I'd finally asked him if he'd move in now, and then we could look for something more permanent at some point. Okay, I hadn't asked, I'd demanded. But hey, once a diva, always a diva.

I'd worried in the beginning that Wren might get bored of living back in a small town, or that he'd get tired of his new job as coach at his old high school, but I'd been wrong. He was thriving, and in the short time he'd already implemented a mentoring program for students to support one another.

I'd met Coach and Mrs. Johnson shortly after the coach retired and had loved hearing all the stories about my gorgeous boyfriend when he was a kid. I'd also had all the warnings from Mrs. Johnson about being a football widow and that knowing how to bake would go a long way.

"Eep!" I screeched when a pair of strong arms enveloped me from behind.

I was turned around, and before I had any warning, Wren's lips consumed me. Fuck, I'd missed him.

"You're never..."—I sucked on his lower lip—"going away..."—groped his ass—"ever..."

A voice cleared and I froze, looking into Wren's eyes, and whispered, "We're not alone."

"No," he whispered back, "but fuck if that isn't the best reception a guy could want."

He kissed me again, this time with a lot less heat, giving my cock a chance to stand down till later.

"Hi, I'm Aiden."

"Oh my god, you're Wren's best friend." I pushed Wren off me and went to give Aiden a big hug.

"Well, I think I've been bumped to second best friend now." He winked.

"Nope, we're naked best friends, that's a different category. You still get first place in the clothed best friend one. Speaking of which, is that what I think it is?"

I couldn't help admire his Valentino jacket. He looked at Wren and mouthed, "I approve."

"Oh, come have a drink. We have all kinds of cocktails. All non-alcoholic, but you'll never notice the difference."

Charlie and Kris arrived shortly after with beaming smiles.

"Did you find a house?"

Charlie leaned into Kris. "Oh my god, Tinker Bell, it's so beautiful like you wouldn't believe it."

I gave them both a hug and then Charlie looked at Kris before giving me a large package.

"What's this?" I asked.

"Just something from Lydovia's biggest artist," Kris said. Love and pride radiating from him as he looked at Charlie.

I took the parcel to the checkout desk and opened it carefully. Wrapped in layers of tissue paper was a hand-drawn image of Coco Chanel.

Tears filled my eyes and I had to step away from the drawing so I wouldn't damage it.

"It's beautiful, Charlie," I managed to say after putting my arms around him again and squeezing him tight.

He was a talented artist, and I was so proud that after meeting Kris he'd been able to make his own dream of becoming an artist come true.

"By the way, who's the hot blond by the door?" I whispered to them.

Kris whispered back, "That's James, our security, and he can hear you. He's also a friend so you don't need to worry."

"Oops." I shrugged.

Wren had gone to help Indy close up Spilled Beans—as in, he'd gone to stand by the door to make sure no one came in for personal advice while he was trying to clean up and close. The amount of times Indy had been late to a dinner or meet up was ridiculous.

My heart skipped a beat as I saw them cross the square toward my store, and then it skipped a beat again when I remembered I *had* a store.

"Hey, has anyone heard from Connor? He said he'd come over for a coffee before the party, but he hasn't turned up."

Everyone shook their heads and some of us checked our cellphones.

"No messages either. I'm still expecting him to make it."

Charlie's cellphone rang and we all looked at him.

"Hey, Hannah, we're at Fabulize...okay." He hung up and seconds later Hannah, Ellie, Ben, and Tristan walked in.

Hannah was the one that spoke first. "I have a friend at the police station. They got a call for a disturbance at an address. He recognized the address because he once dropped me off there. It looks like someone's robbed Connor's place."

The quiet blond guy in the corner, James, approached us and spoke to Hannah very matter-of-factly. "Was he at home at the time of the robbery?"

"No, but he's not answering his calls either," Hannah said.

James put his hand on Kris's arm and they exchanged a look. Kris nodded and James left the store and got in the car that was parked outside.

No one spoke much for a while, and I knew everyone was worried about Connor. I offered my sugary drinks and snacks to keep their hands and heads occupied.

Wren took my hand and nudged me toward the office at the back.

"I know this is meant to be a happy day and now it kinda isn't, but don't forget the amazing work you've done with the store and how proud I am of you, okay?"

I smiled and nodded.

"God, I so want to pull you into one of those fitting rooms and have my way with you." He kissed my lips gently.

"Later," I promised.

Kris's cellphone rang just as we came back out.

"James." We were all on standby for whatever news he had until he relaxed. "Okay. Yeah, stay with him. We'll figure it out."

He hung up the phone with a relieved smile gracing his lips. "Connor is fine. Looks like he was out shopping when the house was broken into. James is staying with him until they know more."

At the end of the evening I'd spoken to so many people I didn't know how I hadn't lost my voice. The pre-opening get together was a success and the people of Chester Falls couldn't wait to have a bespoke appointment at Fabulize to discuss all their stylistic needs.

Wren didn't leave me a single moment, always holding my hand, touching my back, or making sure I had a drink or some food.

Yeah, today was hands down the happiest day of my life, and I couldn't wait for the next happiest day of my life, because with Wren at my side there would be as many as the rainbows in the sky after a rainy day.

Thank you so much for reading *How to Catch a Rival*, the second book in the Chester Falls series. Keep reading to get a special bonus scene.

Did you know Tom almost didn't get his story? When I wrote *How to Catch a Prince*, Tom was just Charlie's roommate but he clearly made an impression on my editor who left a note on the edits asking for Tom's story. And Tom being Tom, he wasn't happy enough to get his story, he had to bump himself all the way up to book two. How cheeky!

Up next is *How to Catch a Bodyguard*. Remember that scene in *How to Catch a Prince* between Connor and James? Find out what's behind that tension in their story.

Be sure to follow me on Bookbub to be notified of new releases, and look for me on Facebook for sneak peaks of upcoming stories.

Please take a moment to write a review of *How to Catch a Rival*. If you leave a review Tom will bake you one of his super rainbow cupcakes with sprinkles and all!

If you would like to be the first to know when my new releases are available, read exclusive FREE stories and know what I'm up to, please sign up for my newsletter, Ana's VIP Readers: *bit.ly/AnaAshley*.

For giveaways, sneak peaks, ARC opportunities and general caffeinated fun times, please join my facebook group! Café RoMMance - Ana's Reader Group.

BONUS SCENE

THE SIX-MONTH ANNIVERSARY

WREN

"Hey, how's it going?" Tristan asked as he approached the bench I sat on in the town square. "I see you do it too."

"Do what?" I asked, already knowing what he was going to say.

"Watch your man from afar."

I looked back toward Fabulize, the fashion store owned by the man who'd stolen my heart just six months ago. Tom was by the window, dressing one of his mannequins. Even from where I sat, I could see the look of concentration on his beautiful face.

Tristan looked at his watch and sat next to me, his gaze on Bookmarked, or rather, on Ben, who was doing something on the checkout computer.

"I love coming here just before closing time and watching Ben as he puts his books back on the shelves or jokes with Ellie about whatever they both find funny."

"It's amazing seeing Tom realize his dream. He always looks so happy, even when I can tell he's tired," I said.

Tristan hummed in agreement. I'd often wondered if the benches in the town square had been strategically placed by someone who wanted the perfect place to watch over a loved one.

"Ben and I are going to O'Mahoney's tonight. Do you and Tom want to join us?" Tristan asked.

"Thanks, maybe next time. It's our six-month anniversary."

"Oh, I see. In that case, congratulations, and have a great time tonight."

Tristan bumped his shoulder against mine before he got up and headed toward Spilled Beans, no doubt to get Ben one of his favorite vanilla-and-cinnamon lattes.

My gaze returned to Tom, who now had a dozen scarves over his shoulder and was trying them on the mannequin, one by one. He was likely talking to his muse, Coco Chanel, under his breath and then agreed the outfit didn't need the scarf.

My chest felt tight with the intensity of my love for him. I looked at the clock on the Town Hall building, standing from the bench as if it had springs when I saw it was one minute past closing time.

Tom was no longer at the front of the store. I wanted a silent entry, but I knew it was impossible because the little bell above the door announced my presence as soon as I opened it.

"I'm sorry, we're—"

Tom didn't finish what he was saying before he jumped into my arms, wrapping his legs around my waist and stealing a kiss from me. His tongue demanded entry into my mouth, which I was more than happy to oblige.

"Angel," I gasped against his lips as he sucked on mine and

then moved to the spot beneath my earlobe that he knew always drove me insane.

I twisted to lock the door and switch the store's main lights off, leaving only the spotlights in the window.

"Say it again," he demanded.

I walked us to the back, where Tom had the best sex couch in the world. His words.

"Angel, my angel. God, I love you so much," I whispered in his ear.

When I'd put together the paperwork for the lease of the shop months ago, I'd found out Tom's middle name was Angel. He'd told me no one had ever called him by his middle name, so he'd almost forgotten he wasn't just Tom.

I'd told him then he would never be *just* anything. He was my Tom, my angel, my love, my everything.

Tom's hands tightened around my shoulders, and he moved his hips to get some friction against his hard cock.

"I love you too, sprinkles."

I chuckled at the ridiculous nickname he'd given me. One kitchen accident, and I was stuck with the name for life. Thank goodness he only used it in private...so far, at least.

He whimpered when I pressed him against a wall halfway to our final destination.

I knew all of Tom's sounds, and that was no regular lust-filled moan.

"Baby, are you wearing a plug?" I asked, pulling my head back to look at him.

His cheeks were adorably flushed as he trapped his lips between his teeth. He nodded.

"Do you remember the store's preopening party?" he asked, his hand moving from my back and his fingers trailing a path from my Adam's apple to the top button on my shirt.

"Yes?"

"Do you remember what you said you'd do?"

I nuzzled Tom's neck, pushing him farther against the wall.

"Uh-huh. I remember. Is that what you want, angel? You want me to fuck you in your fitting room. Right here, in the store where anyone passing by could see?"

"Fuck yes, with a cherry on top."

With Tom in my arms, I walked into the fitting room on the opposite side of the store. When we got inside, Tom unwrapped himself from me to close the heavy curtain that gave his customers privacy to change.

I knew it was unlikely anyone could see us from the street, but with the mirrors Tom had all over the store, it was safer to keep the curtain closed.

Tom placed himself in front of me but facing the floor-to-ceiling mirror. He locked his eyes with mine as his fingers undid each button on his shirt.

When all the buttons were undone, he removed the shirt, giving his hips a slight tilt as if he was putting on a show for me. It was nearly impossible for my cock to not react to Tom, even when we were doing something as innocent as watching TV or making dinner together, but now I was painfully hard, and he knew it.

"Are you going to stand there and watch or are you going to get naked too?" he asked.

"In a hurry, angel?"

"To have your thick cock inside me? You bet your bubble butt I am."

Against his wishes, I didn't get undressed, but I did get on my knees behind Tom, turned him around, and pushed him against the changing room wall. He yelped when his back hit the cold brick wall.

"Keep your eyes on the mirror," I said.

I palmed his erection through the soft fabric of his slacks, but I didn't want to tease him too much. Knowing Tom, he'd been wearing the plug for the best part of the afternoon and was ready to blow, and I didn't want that to happen before I was inside him.

His cock was so hard it nearly hit me in the face when I pulled his slacks and underwear down to his feet. He started lifting his feet to get fully naked, but I held his ankle in place as our eyes met in the mirror.

"Wren."

"I want to taste you, baby," I said, stroking him gently and sucking his balls one at a time, moving slowly up his shaft.

"*Mmph*, stop, please. If you touch me, I'll come," he begged.

I loved that he was so desperate for me. The last six months had been so full of highs that I was still waiting for the other shoe to drop. But it didn't seem it ever would. Tom was simply my perfect match, my teammate.

"Turn around," I said.

He did, arching his back so I had a perfect view of the end of his plug. I stood, fully clothed and flush against him.

When I looked in the mirror, I saw Tom's eyes on us. I brushed my thumb against his nipple, feeling it harden under my touch, and then paid equal attention to the other.

Tom leaned his head back onto my shoulder, his breath ragged. "Please, I need you."

I captured his mouth with mine as I pulled his plug out. I unzipped my jeans, pulled my cock out, and aligned it with his eager hole.

"Look at you, angel," I whispered in his ear, tilting his head so he faced the mirror again.

I pushed my way inside him gently, feeling the slick, tight

heat around my cock and stopping only when I was fully seated.

Tom let out a contented sigh followed by a moan when I sucked a patch of skin on the sensitive spot on the back of his neck.

"I've been waiting to feel your magic cock inside me all day," he said, pulling his hips away from me and pushing back again.

I placed my hand on top of his on the wall and linked our fingers while my other arm went around his waist to keep him in place. I thought he'd use his free hand to jerk himself, but when he put his arm around mine on his waist, I knew what he needed.

"This is going to be fast and hard, baby," I said.

"I'm here for it, with bells on."

After a few slow moves in and out of Tom, I was happy enough that he'd adjusted to my size and increased my pace.

The sounds of flesh hitting flesh echoed around the store alongside Tom's little moans of pleasure. My jeans had ridden down my legs and pooled around my ankles. In the mirror, the reflection of our bodies joined was the most erotic thing I'd seen in my life.

Tom's cock leaked ferociously, and his moans increased in pitch each time I hit his prostate.

"Open your eyes, baby," I said. "I want you to see us. See how beautiful you look, all flushed. You feel so good, angel."

"Wren, please. I need to come. Make me come now or—"

"Or what, angel?" I wanted to laugh at his likely empty threat, but he decided to meet each of my thrusts with his own. "Fuck."

I knew Tom would find a way to turn the tables on me and take control to get to his orgasm faster, and that's what he did.

He stood straight and clenched his muscles around my cock. I kept up the fast pace, knowing this position made it easier to hit his prostate and reach for his cock simultaneously.

Tom reached behind me to put one hand on my thigh to keep me going, and the other went around my neck to pull me in for a kiss.

"I'm so close, Wren. So close."

"Me too, baby."

A few strokes of his cock were all it took. Tom's whole body shook with pleasure, and he released my mouth, giving me the opportunity to watch him in the mirror.

Looking into Tom's beautiful violet eyes, my body stopped being my own. I was as powerless to stop thrusting into his tight channel as I was to control my oncoming orgasm.

"I love you so much, sprinkles," he said as he tried to get his breath back and kiss me.

I slowly pulled out of Tom and sat on the leather seat I hadn't noticed before, taking Tom down with me. "I love you too, angel."

His hair was all over the place, and I was still wearing my shirt. I chuckled. "Talk about getting down and dirty, hey?"

"No one got down, babe, only dirty. And you can fucking do that to me again any time," he said, curling into me. "In fact, I might make it part of my end-of-day procedures. Cash up, tidy up, sex in the fitting room."

As he shivered, I remembered he was fully naked, and my release was leaking from him onto my bare legs.

"Oops." He shrugged but reached under the seat, brought out a box of tissues, and started cleaning us up.

"Why do you have tissues in your fitting room?" I asked.

"You'd be surprised at how often my clients get all emo on me when they see how they look after I Fabulize them."

Once we were clean, we dressed and made sure the room was back to its original state. That included cleaning the floor and wall that Tom had come on so fabulously. Just the thought of it made me hard again.

"Angel, come here," I said, sitting on the comfortable sofa in Tom's office. He was putting some paperwork and designs away before we left the store.

"What's up?" He sat on my lap and ran his hands up and down my chest. "Are you ready to go again? Because I think I need food first, sprinkles."

I laughed and put my hand on the back of his neck to pull him down for a kiss.

"Baby, you turn me on just by existing, but even I need some recovery time."

I took my phone out and tapped the video app. A few seconds later, Gina's face appeared on the screen.

"Hello, my darlings. How are you doing? I hope you're celebrating your anniversary in style."

Tom looked at me and then the screen.

"Hi, G," he said, waving back.

"Angel, I have a gift for you," I said.

"And it's not the one he's just given you," Gina said with a sassy laugh.

Tom's face went an adorable shade of pink. When I'd met Tom, I thought nothing would ever phase him, but in the last six months, I'd learned that he was confident and self-assured, but he was also a super-sweet homebody who was occasionally shy.

"What gift? I don't understand." He leaned farther into me, and I put my free arm around his waist.

Gina flipped the camera, and Tom gasped. "Oh my god. Is that—"

On the small screen was a litter of kittens feeding from their mommy, Cosmo, Gina's cat.

"They're so cute, Gina. You never told me Cosmo was pregnant," Tom said, beaming.

"That's because we didn't know. The sneaky little hussy has been canoodling with the new neighbor's cat," Gina said.

Cosmo looked up at the phone and meowed as if she knew we were talking about her.

"They are adorable, Gina," Tom said.

I kissed his hair and whispered, "Do you want to see your present?"

He lifted his head, his eyes as wide as saucers. It was adorable how he tried to contain his smile just in case he wasn't about to hear what he hoped for.

"Show him, Gina," I said to the phone.

The image moved to where one of Cosmo's kittens was asleep on a colorful scarf, totally ignoring his little brothers and sisters scrambling all over each other to feed.

"Who's that one?"

"That one is ours, baby. Happy anniversary," I said.

"Oh, my holy glitter crickets, are you serious?" He clasped his hands in front of his mouth.

I nodded, and Tom let out the happiest shriek as he bounced up and down on my lap.

"My darlings, I've got to go," Gina said. "Tom, sweetie, I'll come by the store tomorrow. I need a super outfit for a dinner."

"Sure thing. I'll have a cocktail waiting for you. Thank you so much, G."

I put the phone down on the sofa and did what I'd wanted to do the moment I saw Tom's reaction to the baby kitten. I kissed him.

"When can we go see him?"

"Her."

"It's a girl?"

"Yup, we're the proud parents of a girl kitten."

Tom's eyes watered. In one of our post-sex chats, he'd confessed that because he'd grown up in the city, his mom didn't think it was right to have a pet that would be confined to their apartment.

When Gina told me about Cosmo's predicament, my first thought was to fulfill Tom's dream. In the last six months, Tom had worked hard to make his business successful, he'd been there for my first game as coach of the high school football team, and he'd even baked a batch of rainbow cupcakes when the team won their first game of the season.

Tom was perfect. Our life together was perfect, and the kitten was the cherry on top.

"Can I call her Coco?" he asked.

"You'll find it's a very fitting name, angel."

I pulled up the photos Gina had sent me earlier and showed them to Tom. Coco was mostly black with beautiful, shiny fur, but around her neck were white spots that almost looked like a pearl necklace.

"She's so perfect," Tom said. "I've always wanted a pet, and she's so…" His voice broke, and I pulled him into a hug.

"Come on, angel. Let's pick up food from Benny's and go home. I made you a cake."

"With sprinkles?"

"What do you think?"

"I think I must have done something incredible in a previous life to get you in this one."

He stood and held out his hand for me. I followed him as I knew I would: anywhere, everywhere, forever.

PREVIEW OF HOW TO CATCH A BODYGUARD

JAMES

A year ago

I'd always wondered what it would be like to see Connor Williams again. Would his bright green eyes still light up a room? Would he still have the same dusting of freckles over his nose and cheeks, so light that you almost couldn't see them unless you were too close? Would his shiny, copper-colored hair have turned a darker shade as he grew older?

It's not like I'd spent the last fifteen years thinking about him. Well, maybe a little. He was, after all, the first boy I fell for. What I hadn't expected was for the devastating feelings from the last time I'd seen him to come back in full force.

The way he'd looked into my eyes after I'd given him the first and most shattering kiss of my life. It had been so brief, it could barely be considered a kiss, and he hadn't pushed me away or hit me as I'd half expected.

No, he'd just stared at me looking confused. His eyes had

become a dark forest green, and his lips were parted as if he wanted more. God, I'd so wanted more.

But instead, he just whispered, *"You kissed me."* And then he ran.

That same day, my mom told me we were moving, and I never had a chance to talk to Connor again. To say goodbye, to apologize.

Now, staring into those same green eyes, at the same copper-colored hair, I was that fifteen-year-old boy again. The one who had never understood why two such different kids became friends to start with, other than it just had been that way.

Connor had been the popular kid. He'd played football and had had the whole boy-next-door look going for him. I bet he'd even mowed the lawn for his neighbors and delivered newspapers on the weekend.

I'd mostly spent my time at home in the small two-bedroom house I'd shared with my mom in Bethany, a few miles outside of Chester Falls. I'd been skinny and awkward and hadn't understood why the most beautiful boy at school had wanted to be my friend.

The difference between now and then was that, amongst other things, I'd grown into my body. I was no longer the gangly, fifteen-year-old boy Connor had known. And I certainly wasn't the same naive kid that had misunderstood his friend's closeness for attraction.

Warmth rushed through my body as Connor's eyes locked with mine. His brows furrowed, creating a cute V on his forehead. My fingers twitched, wanting things they had no place wanting, such as smoothing out that little crinkle above Connor's nose.

"But first, let me introduce you to Captain James Bennett."

The voice of my friend Kris, the Prince of Lydovia, brought me back into the reason for being here.

"James is my protection detail while I'm in America." Kris carried on as he revealed his identity to his boyfriend Charlie's family. Well, fake boyfriend.

Somehow, since I'd dropped Kris off in Chester Falls, he'd gone and fallen for the gentle Charlie after deciding to stand in as Charlie's boyfriend at his sister Hannah's wedding to her girlfriend, Ellie.

I'd never met Connor's family, and with Charlie having bright red hair, it never occurred to me that they would be related, even though they shared a surname. It was clear now, seeing them in the same room, that they were brothers. Same green eyes, same nose, same freckles.

As a bodyguard, my job was to protect those under my charge, but I'd also been hired for this particular job because I was a friend, and with my Special Ops background, I had the relevant experience, which meant I wasn't just hired muscle.

In fact, what most people aside from Kris didn't know was that my muscle was mainly for show. Yes, I could use my size and my strength in a fight, and I had pretty good aim with a gun, but I didn't like to use either. My strength came from intuition, observation, and analysis before the need for action.

Finding out Connor was Charlie's brother was like a sucker punch to the stomach. My brain worked hard to think of any clues I'd missed, because as Kris and Charlie discussed the ramifications of a press leak, all I could think was what was Connor's role in the whole thing, considering the journalist making the threat was his girlfriend.

Even though my eyes had been looking straight ahead, I'd been keeping an eye on everyone in the family for their reaction. And then, because I was a sucker for punishment, I looked at Connor again.

I couldn't read him, but there was no mistaking the tension in his frame. His forearms were resting on his knees while his hands were fisted in a way I bet caused his nails to dig into his palms, and his gaze remained fixed on the carpeted floor.

Suddenly, he stood up and walked toward the door, but I stepped in his way. He hadn't expected the move because he'd stopped still, mere inches from me. So close, I could feel the warmth from his body through his shirt.

I crossed my arms to give us some distance and make myself look taller, bigger, and stronger. I'd always been just that little bit taller than Connor, but it had never been noticeable as kids because he'd always been bigger thanks to his football training.

It was a dick move, but I couldn't be sure that he wouldn't leave the room to share Kris and Charlie's plans with his girlfriend.

Even though I was six foot ten, Connor was only an inch shorter than me, so it didn't take much for our eyes to meet again.

When they did, it was as though everyone in the room vanished and there was only Connor and I. Two fifteen-year-old friends waiting for the bus while sharing a bag of Skittles and fighting over who got to eat the red ones.

Connor's green eyes were bright, but he also looked exhausted. I don't know how long we stood there staring at each other, but it was long enough for me to revisit the little pattern of freckles under his eyes that looked like star constellations.

I'd always used to joke with him that I could read the horoscope on his face and made up ridiculous predictions based on them. Connor had hated his freckles. He'd said they made him look like a girl, but I'd thought they were perfect, even though I'd never dared say it out loud.

I knew the moment he'd finally recognized me because his eyes opened wider and he took half a step back, his mouth parting slightly and a small breath escaping from between his lips.

Connor looked at the people in the room as though, just like me, he'd only just remembered they were there.

"James," Kris called. "Let him go."

"Kris, you don't know—"

He held his hand up so I had no choice but to follow orders and let Connor leave the room.

I hoped Kris's trust in Connor wasn't misplaced because I wasn't so sure, especially when, not thirty minutes later, a knock on the door announced the arrival of Connor and his girlfriend, Ceecee Bloomfield, the journalist who was trying to leak both Kris's location and Charlie's identity to the general public.

What followed was the kind of crisis management and planning I'd only ever seen before a deployment.

The Williams family had rallied around Kris and Charlie like a protective shield of love. It was clear to everyone that Kris and Charlie had fallen head over heels for each other, even if the family didn't know the whole thing had started off as fake.

Twenty-four hours later, not only had I been proven wrong about Connor, but I'd seen his loyalty to his brother and his family in the way he'd put his own heartbreak aside to support them.

Ceecee had come through on her promise to keep the story out of the press until the end of the wedding, but I still didn't trust her. So, despite Charlie's mom's kind invite to join the wedding party, I wasn't ready to face Connor again.

Sticking to checking the perimeter of the hotel in order to avoid bumping into Connor didn't do me any good when I turned a corner around a tall hedge in the garden and nearly bumped into him.

"Watch where—" He stopped as soon as he saw it was me.

I stood there not knowing what to say, but when the silence between us became too heavy to handle, I simply said, "Hi."

"Hi," he said.

More silence. I hated silence.

"Connor," I said, even though I didn't know what would follow next.

"Nice to see you again, James," Connor said as he walked off.

The last time he'd done it, I'd wanted to chase after him. This time, I knew not doing it was for the best.

My body's reaction to seeing him, despite everything, told me my heart wasn't safe around Connor.

"Goodbye, Con," I whispered to myself as if the statement would bear more weight if it was out in the world.

It didn't matter anyway. My last deployment would start as soon as Kris was back in Lydovia, and then it was anyone's guess as to where in the world I'd end up.

CONNECT WITH ANA

Connect with Ana on social media:

Hang out in my FB Group:
facebook.com/groups/CafeRoMMance
Follow me on instagram: *instagram.com/anawritesmm/*
Follow me on Bookbub: *bookbub.com/authors/ana-ashley*
Sign up to my newsletter: *bit.ly/AnaAshley*

For an overview of all of Ana's books and audiobooks, visit her website: *anawritesmm.com/books*

BOOKS BY ANA ASHLEY

Single Dads of Stillwater
A spin off series from Chester Falls that can be read on its own. Each book features one or more single dads in this community of friends, family and found family. In this contemporary MM romance series you'll find heat, emotion and a guaranteed happy ever after.
Newcomer
Antagonist
Breakthrough
Heartstring
Datebook (Coming early 2024)

Finding You Series
A standalone series set across the Atlantic between New York and Portugal. Find your way home with this contemporary MM romance series with friends to lovers, star-crossed lovers and age gap with plenty of heat, feels and always a happy ever after.
Home Again
Together Again
Love Again
And for a special short story, Complete Again, plus bonus scenes, grab the Finding You boxset now.

Room for 3 series
This is a high heat MMM contemporary romance series set in an island resort.
The Resort
The Vacation (Free short story)

Chester Falls Series
From a Prince to a Happy Ever After for all, enjoy this small town MM romance series that's as sweet as they come, with plenty of heat, humor and everything in between.
How to Catch a Bookworm (Prequel short)

How to Catch a Prince
How to Catch a Rival
How to Catch a Bodyguard
How to Catch a Bachelor
How to Catch the Boss (a Christmas novella)
How to Catch a Biker
How to Catch a Vet
How to Catch a Happy Ever After
You can now have all the books in the series and the prequel all in two boxsets.
Chester Falls Collection Volume I
Chester Falls Collection Volume II

Standalone books
Christmas Bubble: a low angst, standalone, Christmas novel featuring a petite but larger-than-life cheerleader, an older demisexual football coach and a winter cabin by the lake with only one bed. With cameos from Chester Falls and Stillwater.
Midnight Ash: a sweet Cinderella fairytale retelling with a sexy kinky twist on the side, and a cast who don't quite behave as you'd expect.
Stronghold: a sweet and sexy romance in Sarina Bowen's World of True North, Vino & Veritas series. This is a standalone story between two childhood friends who reunite after as decade apart, with some creative use of maple syrup.

FREE READS
My Fake Billionaire
The Vacation

ABOUT ANA

Ana Ashley was born in Portugal but has lived in the United Kingdom for so long, even her friends sometimes doubt if she really is Portuguese.

After getting hooked on reading gay romance, Ana decided to follow her lifelong dream of becoming an author.

These days you can find her in front of her laptop bringing her stories to life, or in the kitchen perfecting her recipe for the famous Portuguese custard tarts.

Ana Ashley writes sweet and steamy gay romance set in America, often in small towns where everyone knows everyone.

You can follow Ana on the usual social media hangouts.

For access to exclusive teasers, content, and general book and food related goodness you can now join Ana in her Facebook Group, Café RoMMance - Ana's Reader Group

Ana's VIP Readers - bit.ly/AnaAshley

Facebook Page - @anawritesmm

Email - ana@anaashley.com

Instagram - @anawritesmm

Bookbub - bookbub.com/authors/ana-ashley

Goodreads - goodreads.com/ana-ashley

www.ingramcontent.com/pod-product-compliance
Lightning Source LLC
Chambersburg PA
CBHW020754190726
48285CB00006B/2022